Alan Hunter was born in 1922 in Hoveton St John on the River Bure near Norwich, where he also grew up. After an early spell of poultry farming, he spent the war years in the RAF and subsequently worked as a bookseller in Norwich for 10 years. He has been a regular reviewer of fiction for the *Eastern Daily Press* for the past 20 years.

Alan Hunter now lives in the Broads; he is married and has a daughter.

Also by Alan Hunter in Futura

ALAN HUNTER

Gently Between Tides

Futura

A Futura Book

Copyright © Alan Hunter 1982

First published in Great Britain in 1982
by Constable & Company Ltd

This edition published in 1985
by Futura Publications, a Division of
Macdonald & Co (Publishers) Ltd
London & Sydney

ISBN 0 7088 2686 5

Printed and bound in Great Britain by
Collins, Glasgow

Futura Publications
A Division of
Macdonald & Co (Publishers) Ltd
Maxwell House
74 Worship Street
London EC2A 2EN

A BPCC plc Company

Though they were having a fine spell that October, there was still a heavy mist on the river at 10 a.m., and the workboat coming up on the last of the high water slack was nosing its way cautiously from marker to marker.

All you could really see were sodden banks that appeared and vanished in an illogical way, while the mist was damp and nipping, smelling of mud and decayed vegetation. The markers were simple willow wands, showing where the deep-water channel lay. Elsewhere, even at high water, mud shoals waited to trap the unwary.

The boatman, a hunched figure, had an unlit pipe jammed in his mouth. As he stared ahead with narrowed eyes he could feel the wet hoar on his eyebrows. A heron, getting up suddenly, startled him, for he hadn't seen it standing so still in a drain; it wheeled above him on broad wings and drops from its dangling legs fell in the boat. He muttered a curse and straightened the tiller, which he had jerked askew in his surprise. The heron vanished spectrally into the mist; it was the only living thing he had seen.

The boat pottered on. At any time now one should see timber piles looming up to port, then the ghosts of buildings, a mast, and finally the span of a stone bridge. Only they seemed such a long time appearing, as though the mist had somehow swallowed them up! Yet, by the boatman's computation, he had turned the last bend below the quay. He felt a moment of panic. Could he have gone wrong, perhaps getting himself into one of the drains? But that was scarcely possible; he had followed the wands attentively, keeping each one to starboard.

Suddenly he hit his reverse with a shout, setting water rumbling beneath the workboat. Drab in the mist, and almost on top of him, loomed a varnished dinghy with an outboard motor. It was drifting sideways, plumb in his course, and the workboat halted only just in time.

'What bloody fool . . . !'

He lumbered forward, intent to catch the dinghy before it drifted off; but arriving at the bows, he stiffened, gazing down into the dinghy with incredulous eyes.

He was looking at a woman, and the woman was dead. About that there could be no shadow of doubt. She was lying tumbled on the floorboards, her face waxen, her clothes sodden by the mist. The face was turned upwards, its eyes staring, lips parted over the teeth; and on her throat was livid bruising. The poor bitch had been strangled.

'God almighty . . . !'

The boatman came out of his trance in time to catch the dinghy's painter. Hissing through his teeth, he worked the dinghy round until he could loop the painter over his towing post. Then he stood staring at the woman, still trying to believe what he was seeing.

Meanwhile the workboat's engine went on burbling to itself in neutral, and somewhere in the mist, seeming quite close, one could hear the sound of vehicles passing on a road.

It was a Saturday, and the boatman was on overtime; normally, he would have gone into town for the football.

'I'll get it, Mr George.'

On the landing at Heatherings, Gently was putting the last touches of paint on the rails, drawing the brush in voluptuous strokes to give the balustrade a perfect finish. The Jonsons had been content to have the paintwork brown, no doubt under the impression that it was more 'period', but Gabrielle had at once decided that it made the hall too dark. The hall, which was the size of a large room, rose to the height of the second storey ceiling: there had been plenty to do. This was the second weekend that Gently had been toiling away at it.

'If it's for me, say I'm busy.'

It was Mrs Jarvis who was trotting over to the phone, leaving open a door from which issued a smell of roast pork to mingle with the heavy smell of paint.

Mrs Jarvis was in her element. At first, it had seemed like the end of the world when Gently had got married, making redundant the villa at Finchley where, as a bachelor, he had lived for so long. With a fancy French wife he didn't need a housekeeper, and suddenly Mrs Jarvis's future had seemed a blank: her husband long dead, her daughter married, and the house that was her home about to be sold . . .

Then they had asked her, very tentatively, whether she wouldn't consider keeping house at Heatherings, to live in there while they were away so that the place shouldn't be unoccupied. Well, she'd had her doubts – her, a Londoner! – but they had vanished when they took her to see it. Soon she was installed with her precious bits and pieces and lording it over a daily help and a gardener.

Gently had never seen her so chirpy, or, for that matter, more bossy.

'Who is it – Reymerston?'

'No, it's one of your lot, Mr George. Says he's sorry if you're busy, but could you spare him five minutes.'

'Tell him to hang on.'

Sighing, he looked round for somewhere to put his brush, then scrubbed his painty fingers on overalls already well-daubed. This was a bachelor weekend: Gabrielle was in France, and not due back until late the next evening. What he wanted was to get the hall done so that he could say to her at the door:

'Close your eyes . . .'

In other words, he wasn't in the mood for any interruptions from 'his lot'.

'Gently here.'

'Ah, Superintendent . . . I'm Tom Bedingfield, the county Chief Constable. Let me begin by saying how pleased I was to hear that you were coming to live this way . . .'

Groaning to himself, Gently hooked up a chair and dropped on it. Sir Thomas was only the latest of a number of such callers since they had arrived at Heatherings. The local paper had done a feature, and after that the phone had started ringing: people who had wanted to meet him, and, even more, Gabrielle.

'I know the house you've bought, in fact I was acquainted with Colonel Jonson . . . a lovely place . . . I couldn't want to see it fall into better hands. Is Mrs Gently there?'

'She's in France.'

'Ah. I was going to beg an introduction. You're on your own then?'

'I'm on my own.'

Was the fellow about to invite him to dinner?

'Well . . . aha! . . . why I'm ringing, apart from my wanting to say hallo . . . the fact is, I have a small problem. You have met Inspector Leyston, haven't you?'

'I've met him.'

'Well, it's like this. There has been an incident at Thwaite Maltings . . . a woman dead in a boat, thought to have been strangled some time yesterday. Well, I want to put in some extra talent, but Leyston is being obstinate. It's his case, and he wants to keep it, but I'm not sure he has the resources to handle it. I have every confidence in him and all that, but Shinglebourne is hardly a metropolis . . .'

It wasn't. It was the sort of place you didn't know whether to call a town or a village, mostly a single street strung along beside a stony beach. And Leyston, he'd be verging on retirement, a sombre, long-featured man with sideboards. A Victorian sort of figure: he went in for black suits with waistcoats, and black Oxford shoes.

'You'll have to overrule him.'

'Aha . . . yes! But I don't quite like doing that. Not at this end of his career, when he has only six months to go. Better if he went off with a flourish, eh? Actually, I've got myself into a predicament. He has rather a high opinion of you, and I suggested that, with you on the spot . . .'

Gently scowled at the phone. Oh no! This sort of thing needed stamping on promptly. Why did they think he had moved out here, if it hadn't been to slam the office door?

'Are you there?'

'I'm here.'

At the other end, harmonics! 'Oh dear, I'm afraid I've put my foot in it, and I was only trying to find an acceptable solution.'

'London will send you a man.'

'Of course. But I was trying to keep it unofficial – just a little chat between you and Leyston, a few pointers, that sort of thing. Leyston will be happy with that, but he won't be happy with a man from London. But naturally I can see your point of view, and perhaps it was unreasonable to suggest it . . .'

Devil take the man! Across the hall, Mrs Jarvis was hovering curiously, her sharp-featured, unsmiling face topped with a tightly-bandaged scarf. It was just on lunchtime. With Gabrielle away, Mrs Jarvis was indulging in a 'proper' lunch – roast pork, dumpling and veg., followed by an apple turnover and custard. Years had taught her that her best-laid plans could be brought to nought by a ring on the phone – yet, out here they ought to be safe. Her eyes were fixed on him indignantly.

'Where is Leyston now?'

'At Shinglebourne. Apparently the woman comes from there. But that's only twenty minutes' drive from your place, so he could be with you in no time at all.'

But what use was that?

'Thwaite was where they found her?'

'Yes – do you know it? It's four miles from Shinglebourne, some big maltings by the river, one of them converted into a concert hall. The boat was found drifting a short distance downstream. The body's gone to Ipswich.'

'Who was she?'

'That's interesting. A naturalised Czech, according to Leyston. Her father defected in the 'fifties. He's a violinist, and plays with the London Philharmonic.'

'She lived with him?'

'She's a divorcee. She lived in the Martello Tower at Shinglebourne.'

Gently hesitated. 'Is there a political angle?'

'Good lord, no! Or I'd be ringing Special.

Gently stared through the window, where, in thin sunlight, butterflies were basking on tall Michaelmas daisies: along with the Red Admirals and Tortoiseshells he could glimpse the scalloped wings of a Comma. It wasn't so easy to say no, here in this county he was adopting, where he would have liked, at least, to have got off on the right foot. At the same time . . .

'Tell Leyston I'll have a word with him after lunch.'

'All I can say to that is thank you. You're getting me off a bit of a hook.'

'I'll meet him at the concert hall car park at Thwaite.'

'I really am most grateful. I promise you I won't put upon you again, and listen, some time when it is convenient . . .'

Gently hung up, and went to clean his brushes. Had he really done the right thing? One thing was certain – the case was Leyston's, and he wasn't going to take it off the jealous local Inspector! He had been on a case with Leyston before and was familiar with the set-up . . . in fact, one of the earliest phone calls at Heatherings had been from the Shinglebourne doctor, Dr Capel.

With Capel, it might be worth having a chat about any goings-on at Shinglebourne.

'Are you going out, Mr George?'

The table at lunch seemed lonely. In the evening, he'd be phoning Gabrielle – would he have the courage to admit to her what he was doing?

'I'll probably be back again for tea.'

Mrs Jarvis sniffed as she collected the dishes.

Outside, when he went to get out his car, it was a still, serene October day.

He found Leyston waiting by his car in a park unexpectedly full of vehicles, and beside which, on a wide, level grass plot, people were picnicking and children playing.

The Maltings stood distant from the village; part of them, by the road, were still functioning, and there a lorry stood under a chute and one heard a rumble of machinery. But at the back another huge brick-and-slate structure had been adapted as a concert hall, one famous for its acoustics and the centre of an annual music festival.

One drove over a big hump-backed bridge below which flowed a tidal river between dishevelled banks, turned left through a yard, then came to the car park, shaded by willows. To the right was the concert hall with, before it, a big bronze sculpture by a celebrated artist; it was popular with visitors, some of whom were posing with it for photographs. Then there was a craft shop in a corner of the car park, which was bounded by a quay where barges once had unloaded. For the rest, a wide view over marshes, with the roofs of the village at a distance.

The mast of a yacht projected above the quay, and a workboat was tethered near it.

'Get in beside me.'

Gently had parked with his bonnet towards the picnic-ground. Beyond it one could see a sweep of the river spreading between mudflats, islets, reeds.

Somehow the scene was as serene as the day, and as innocent as the picnic parties – you couldn't begin to connect it with violent crime. Just a pleasant place on a pleasant Saturday.

'Do you know where it happened?'

'That's just the trouble. It could have happened anywhere down the river.'

Sideboards, waistcoat and all, Leyston was exactly as Gently remembered him. A tall, narrow man with an anxious expression on his pale face, and a slightly irritable manner: Old Muttonchops, Capel called him.

'Did you know her?'

'There aren't many people I don't know in Shinglebourne. She and her husband, as he then was, converted the old Martello Tower. Name of Stoven. He's an architect who lives in London, at Chigwell. Then, after the divorce, she came down here to live. That was a couple of years ago. She'd have an allowance from him, I reckon, and she did part-time work as a book-keeper.'

'She lived alone?'

'As far as I know. A good-looking woman in her early thirties.'

'Any boy friends?'

'None I've heard of.'

'Have you contacted her ex-husband?'

'Chigwell are trying to get on to him, but it seems he's away today.'

'What about her father?'

'Stefan Makovrilov.' Leyston brought out the name with care. 'He lives at Chelsea. But he's away too, playing with his orchestra in Edinburgh.'

'How long had she been dead?'

'Forensic reckon not later than 5 p.m. yesterday.'

'Where was she last seen alive?'

'Going towards the yacht club moorings, which was where she kept her boat, at around 2 p.m.'

'Have you a picture?'

Leyston opened a briefcase and took out a postcard-size photograph. It was in colour, and showed a handsome woman with golden-blonde hair and large green eyes. She had high-cheekboned features and a rather wide jaw and her mouth was smiling, but not her eyes. A watchful, slightly withdrawn expression. You couldn't guess what she might have been thinking.

'Did you ever speak to her?'

'I never had occasion to.'

'Do you know if she had many friends?'

'I haven't had time to enquire much, yet.'

Gently mused over the photograph. The smile that the eyes didn't share was troubling, like the smile of the Mona Lisa: and here made somehow more enigmatic by the Middle-European bone structure. But perhaps it was just a trick of the camera, or a momentary anxiety on the part of the sitter.

'Do you know who her doctor was?'

'Capel. We found his card in a bureau.'

Already he was taking it for granted that it would be he, and not Leyston, who talked to Capel.

'Now . . . first things first! Where's the boat?'

'That's it pulled out down the bank. But it was drenched with dew, and the only dabs were on the outboard, and they were hers.'

They got out and walked down the bank, past picnickers who barely spared them a glance. Hadn't it got round that, earlier that day, a body had been found near the spot?

The dinghy was a twelve-footer with red plastic cushions taped to the seats. An Evinrude outboard motor perched on the transom and there were also oars, laid beneath the seats.

'She was lying in the bottom, sprawled out . . . you could see at once what had happened. She was wearing a skirt and blouse and a woollen cardigan, all soaking. I helped them lift her out. She was stiff as a board.'

'A handbag?'

'There was forty quid in it and some change in a purse, then the usual sort of stuff, compact, lipstick, fags, keys. There was a letter from her father, but it isn't written in English, and a note making an appointment, but signed only with a C.'

'What sort of an appointment?'

'I'll show it to you. Only you can't tell if there's any connection.'

Gently stooped to raise the floorboards, but under them were only dead leaves.

'Is the man who found her about?'

'Yes, I made him hang on. He came up to tow in the yacht.'

They went back to the quay. With the ebb nearly run, the yacht was ten or twelve feet below them. Leyston shouted down. A man in gumboots came out of the yacht and clambered up some iron rungs.

'This is Ted Brinded from Friday's Yard.'

A bulky, red-faced man, he stared at them with anxious, small blue eyes.

'Look, old partners, if I don't get away I'm going to miss this blinking tide . . .'

He was wearing a thick turtle-necked sweater and stained serge trousers, stuffed into the gumboots.

'Just a few questions! Point out where you found the boat.'

'Well, it was just down there, wasn't it? Not above a couple of hundred yards from the bridge.'

'Was the painter trailing?'

'No, it wasn't. Somebody had thrown it into the boat. So like that she was set adrift deliberate and didn't just drag her moorings, like.'

'Where would you say it happened?'

'Now you're asking, but she was coming up on the flood. If it happened some time yesterday, I'd reckon it wasn't too far from here. Look down there.'

He pointed a thick finger towards the marshes and flats downstream, to where, on a long, stretching promontory, one could see a flint tower half-hidden by trees.

'That's Bodney church. There's a sharp turn there where the channel goes north for half a mile. Nothing'll drift past it, ebb or flood, so she couldn't have come from below the church. Leastways, that's my opinion. She stuck on the ebb and came back on the flood.'

'Are there moorings down there?'

'There's a bit of bank where you could pull up a boat.'

'Any houses?'

'No houses, but there's a road running close at the back there.'

'Could you take us there?'

'Look . . . have a heart! I'll be punching the flood as it is . . .'

But Gently was obstinate. In the end, they climbed down the rungs into the workboat, Brinded started the engine and cast off, and soon they were sliding down between the high, oozy banks.

The river bore right, past the frontage of the concert hall, then by the grounds of some private property; there, at the top of a muddy slipway, a sailing-dinghy sat on chocks.

'Who owns that?'

Leyston stared at it doubtfully.

'Reckon that would be the Group Captain's,' Brinded said.

'That'll be his house, back there. He used to have a yacht down at the club.'

'Who is the Group Captain?'

'Group Captain Riddlesworth. He's a big man around Thwaite.'

'He's chairman of the concert hall committee,' Leyston explained. 'He flew bombers during the war. He's a V.C.'

'Are there any other boats moored at Thwaite?'

'Not regular like,' Brinded said. 'You get a yacht or two coming up. Mostly they moor at the club.'

They chuntered on, between reaching grey mudflats and reeds left high by the receding water. In the drains shelduck dabbled, and waders rose from the flats in front of them.

To the left was a wilderness of marsh and drains with the distant dry land invisible; to the right, over flats and reed islets, a low bluff followed the line of the river.

Then, when they turned another bend, a soggy shore appeared, guarded by flats.

'Is this the place?'

'Further up, old partner. You can't get a boat in just here.'

They were passing down a long, straight reach, barred ahead by the church on its promontory. For a while the low bluff was concealed by oaks and by trees that were beginning to colour; but finally the trees ended and there the bluff was covered with gorse.

'You want to go in?'

Brinded throttled down, edging the boat towards the shore. They had come to a short stretch of bank free of flats, where water extended to rough, sodden marsh. They touched, and Brinded jumped ashore.

'Now you can't be long, old partners . . .'

Leyston followed Gently as he sploshed over the marsh to a stretch of rabbit-bitten turf beyond.

'What do you reckon?'

'I don't reckon anything.'

Gently was staring about the spot. It was certainly remote. There was only the church, quarter of a mile away, lost in its trees. The turf was bounded by the gorse, a thick covert, through which however a path led; he followed it, and came to a narrow road only seventy yards from the bank. Though the road was narrow, there was a bit of verge running alongside the gorse.

'A car has parked here . . .'

He pointed to a spot on the verge where the grass was flattened.

'Where does the road go?'

'To Harford,' Leyston said. 'It's the back road from Thwaite.'

'What's at Harford?'

'It's a village down the river, about four miles below Shingle-bourne. There's a yard and moorings there.'

'About the same distance downstream as Thwaite is up-stream . . .'

They returned to the bank, where Brinded waited impatiently. But still Gently wasn't going to be hurried. Slowly, he strolled up and down the turf in the neighbourhood of the workboat. Finally he beckoned to Leyston.

'Look.'

Jammed into the turf was a damp cigarette-end, and, a short distance away, a second. There was also a single expired book-match.

'Was there a book of matches in the handbag?'

Leyston stared blankly; then nodded.

'Do you remember the make?'

He didn't remember either the make of the matches or the cigarettes.

'Pick them up . . .'

It wasn't proof yet, but suddenly Gently felt quite certain: this was the spot. Twenty-four hours ago, under the same kindly sun . . . Why had she come there? One had only to look round. This was a place to meet a lover: remote, unobserved, and with the friendly gorses waiting.

She had moored her dinghy, and sat there during the smoking of two cigarettes. And then . . .

Had her lover come by car, or by boat?

'Get some men out here for a thorough search – especially up there in the gorses. And chase up people who may have seen a car parked there yesterday. Also anyone who has seen boats of any description on this bit of river.'

'Yes, sir.'

For the moment, Leyston had completely forgotten that Gently was unofficial – and Gently, he'd forgotten too, had momentarily taken the case into his hands.

He lit his pipe, and had a last look round before sploshing back again to the workboat. To push off, Brinded had to get his shoulder under the stem and shove till his gumboots almost disappeared. When he jumped aboard, mud flew. Gently waited for him to get under weigh.

'Where were you at 2 p.m. yesterday?'

'Me?' Brinded's blue eyes widened. 'At the yard, wasn't I, having my lunch.'

'That was when the lady fetched her dinghy from the yacht club.'

'Well, I wasn't there to see her, old partner.'

'Wouldn't you have heard the engine?'

He shook his head. 'I was in the top shed, larking with the others.'

'Try to think. I want to know if she set off upstream or down. If you could remember hearing an engine . . .'

Brinded scowled in thought, but, after all, could only shake his head.

A man was waiting for them at the quay. He caught their ropes, looping them deftly over bollards; then he stood by, puffing at a cheroot, while Gently and Leyston clambered up the rungs.

'I'm Riddlesworth. I'd like a word with you.'

He was a short but sturdily built man, determined in manner, but his square features savagely marked by cosmetic surgery. He wore a blazer on the pocket of which was an RAF badge, and a firmly knotted service tie.

'I knew Hannah, you understand. She kept the books for the yacht club . . . who am I talking to?'

He had thrusting, yellow-hazel eyes and a bold chin; but his mouth, no doubt due to the surgery, was a wry, thin slit.

'It has been a shock, I don't mind telling you. I trust you're on the track of the devil who did it. I've met her father, too . . . a fine man. Poor fellow, he'll be devastated.'

Gently said: 'You have something to tell us?'

'What? No, but I'm ready to give you any help. Just ask. I might know something, or be able to do something.'

'Were you out on the river yesterday?'

The yellow eyes gazed steadily from the frozen face.

'No. I've given up my yacht . . . a touch of screws in my old age.'

'Don't you have a dinghy?'

'That's Mark's – my son's.'

'Was he out in it yesterday?'

'No. He's a student at the music school here, he had classes till after five.'

'Does anyone else use it?'

'Susan does sometimes – that's my wife. But not yesterday. Yesterday, she was up at the church arranging flowers.'

He drew on the cheroot, his mouth puckering oddly.

'Look – any time you think I can help you! My house is just up the road. I knew Hannah, you see, which makes it personal.'

'How well did you know her?'

'What –? Now don't start getting any ideas! I knew her to say hallo to at the club, have a drink at the bar, that's all.' He puffed a few times. 'She didn't have many friends . . . rather a reticent type, you'd say. Still felt she was a foreigner, probably. She'd just be pleasant and leave it at that. Are you on to anyone?'

Gently said nothing. Below, the workboat's engine grumbled afresh. When there was a shout from Brinded to cast off, it was Riddlesworth who gave Leyston a hand with the ropes. The engine throttled up. Slowly the tall mast of the yacht drew away from the quay, the workboat came into view, and finally the yacht, gliding obediently on a taut towrope.

'Who does she belong to?'

'A fellow from Cambridge. Brought her round from Maldon last weekend.'

A stocky figure, Riddlesworth stood watching as the two boats slid away down the narrow channel.

'Well, that's it – I've said my say. I won't hold you up any longer.'

He paused, as though expecting Gently to detain him, then turned and walked stiffly away across the park.

'He's like that,' Leyston muttered. 'Always ready to poke his oar in.'

The yacht and the workboat had turned the bend, and now one saw only the moving mast. On the grass plot the picnic parties were packing up, there being a little chill in the afternoon.

2

If Leyston was, as claimed, an admirer of Gently's, he was letting little of it past his face; it might be that he was remembering that moment on the bank when, briefly, he had slipped into a subordinate role. Gently was unofficial. It was probably with reluctance that Leyston had accepted the Chief Constable's compromise, willing to admit as a lesser evil this conference with a Central Office expert. But a conference it was to have been . . .

With an air of injury Leyston lit a cigarette, and then, without another word, went to call up the station and to order out a team to search the bank.

'If you're ready to leave . . .'

They drove to the police station with Leyston's Escort preceding Gently's Princess. A slight haze of mist hung about the fields and trees that here and there showed tints of yellow. The road passed through heath outside Shinglebourne, and there the bracken was red-brown, almost maroon, while a horse-chestnut in a town garden was already shedding big, apricot-coloured leaves.

'May I use your phone?'

Leyston's office had been repainted, but otherwise had changed little. It still smelled of soot, and the desk and chairs were of a pattern reaching back at least fifty years.

Leyston's first move had been to unlock a filing-cabinet and to take from it a handbag to which a label had been tied; he had decanted the contents on his desk, and now sat glumly gazing at them.

'Can I speak to Doctor Capel?'

'I'm sorry, he's out, but if you wish to make an appointment . . .'

It was Tanya, Capel's wife, who was answering, and Gently could imagine her bright face and hyacinth eyes.

'Will you tell him I'll be calling on him later . . . this is Chief Superintendent Gently.'

'Oh . . . it's you! It's a funny thing, but only at lunch Henry was saying . . .'

Meanwhile there had been a tap on the door and a uniformed sergeant had entered. He was carrying a message slip, which he handed silently to Leyston. Leyston scanned it with a faint frown.

'It's a message from forensic. She'd had intercourse a short time before death. No signs of violence on the body, other than bruising to the throat . . . nothing recovered from the nails. Clothing intact, no pregnancy.'

A rendezvous it had been.

'Do those cigarettes and matches square with what we found?'

'Yes – Benson and Hedges. The matches are Bryant and May.'

But still it wasn't absolute proof, though the double conjunction made it almost so: the two brands were common enough, and sometimes coincidences did happen.

'Get them off for saliva tests and matching.'

Gently pored over the contents of the handbag. Among them were the two letters, one addressed in a neat script and the other in a handwriting bold and large. From the latter envelope he took a single sheet.

'That's the note I was telling you about.'

Though its message was short, the large, swaggering handwriting occupied almost the whole sheet:

Hannah –
All right for tomorrow!!! I'll be
on the look out for you.
                                        Chick

There was no date, and the postmark on the envelope was a mere smudge.

'Has this been dusted?'

'We got her prints off it, and a couple of others. But they were smeared.'

'The postmark looks like that of a village post office.'

Leyston merely fingered a sideboard.

'Try it on your local post office.'

Gently was frowning: somewhere, the nickname 'Chick' touched a chord in his memory – and that swirling, exhibition-ist handwriting, hadn't he seen that before, too? It must have been several years ago, and almost certainly not in these parts. But his recall failed him; in any case, there was probably no connection . . .

'Do you reckon it was chummie who wrote the note?'

Gently grunted – that was the tempting interpretation! Hannah Stoven had kept a rendezvous, and in her handbag was a letter confirming just that. But without a date, who could tell? The other letter was dated ten days earlier. She might have kept the note in her handbag for as long, and 'Chick' might even be a woman.

'One thing is certain, she had a boy friend – and it shouldn't be too hard to turn him up. Check with her place of work, the yacht club, neighbours. You're sure to find someone ready to gossip.'

'Where she lived, she didn't have any neighbours.'

True; Gently had seen the Martello Tower. It stood at the end of a causeway to the south of the town, overlooking both the sea and the river. A lonely place. As a holiday home it had no doubt seemed desirable, but as a permanent residence? On the dark winter nights, when the wind howled, and the sea pounded at her very doorstep?

Perhaps she had stuck to the tower because it reminded her of happier days; or perhaps it suited some quirk in her nature.

'Dispatch this stuff, then we'll look the place over.'

Leyston found a form and began scribbling. Through his

window one saw the High Street and the Saturday shoppers, many come in from the outlying villages.

Tied together as though by a wire, two U.S. assault-planes skated in from the sea, angular but comely aircraft, heading for their base a few miles inland. Then across in Friday's Yard, quarter of a mile away, two men were shoring up a hauled-out yacht; otherwise, a gaggle of gulls were the only living things near the squat brick tower.

You drove down the High Street, then past the yard and the yacht club moorings, in the bend of the river, and over broken tarmac that became crunching shingle when you had climbed the ramp to the causeway. At this end a few cars were parked and the dark shapes of anglers were strung along the tideline. Further on, the deep shingle became treacherous, causing car wheels to spin and dig in.

And finally you came to the Martello Tower, which was reached by a footbridge across a dry moat.

Beyond it, for ten miles, stretched a narrow spit of sand dunes, barely separating the river from the sea.

'How long had she lived here?'

'Two years, about.'

So she had seen two winters come and go: in the dark nights, leaving behind the bright town for this brick fortress, lashed by wind.

'Had she a car?'

'No.'

With a torch she must have come down that lonesome track, unlocking the little door across the footbridge to enter rooms probably unheated . . .

The footbridge was closed by a padlocked gate, for which Leyston produced a key. When he had opened the door they went through the thickness of the wall into a short passage, then into a room. It was furnished as a lounge, with a tiny window piercing the wall towards the sea, and struck one at once with a chillness and a certain dank smell. Yet the furniture was bright and modern. On the walls were pictures, landscapes. A bookcase, standing awkwardly against the curvature of the wall, contained books on art and music along with paperback fiction. There was a music stand, and a violin lay with a bow on top of the bookcase. The room had gas lighting and a portable gas stove stood pushed into a corner.

'Through here, there's the bedroom.'

It was a corner cut off by a dividing wall, a circular section with one straight side and a window even smaller than that in the lounge. A single bed had a bright, peasant-y bedspread, and a dressing-table and wardrobe huddled close together. Gently opened the latter: she'd gone in for print dresses and full skirts with embroidered hems.

Other corners formed a kitchen, where she'd cooked on a pressure stove, and a toilet with a shower: at least the tower ran to plumbing.

But everywhere was the dank chillness, reminiscent of a church. Steps led down to an empty basement, others to the flat roof.

'Could you have lived here?'

Gently shrugged and felt for his pipe. The silence of the rooms was tomb-like, the walls being at least six foot thick. Yet still there was a touch of gaiety about the place, bright covers, an amusing carpet: just a little exotic and un-English. Many of the books were in Czech.

He picked up a framed photograph that stood on the bureau: it depicted the girl and, presumably, her father. He was slighter than she; had a bush of greying hair, but the same high cheekbones, though with a narrower jaw. His dark eyes were mischievous. He was wearing a summer shirt, she a print dress, showing off a fine figure.

'Have you been through the bureau?'

'She had some money tucked away, fifteen hundred in her current account. Then three thousand more in a building society. The letters are all from her father.'

So she hadn't been hard up.

'What about the ex-husband?'

'She was getting two hundred a month from him. I found his

address in an address book, but all the other entries are London addresses.'

'Show it to me.'

Leyston produced it. In fact the entries were very few, and clearly belonging to an earlier period. Her father had a flat in Old Church Street.

'Surely she had some friends about here.'

Gently picked up the fiddle, and tried it. The sawing notes he produced sounded keenly in the vault-like stillness. Music on the stand was mazurkas, waltzes: you could imagine that room vibrant with music. And was it just for herself she had played, alone, evoking the gay rhythms of cafés and dance halls?

A patient on Capel's list . . . Capel, who ran the Shingle-bourne Quartet . . .

If she had had talent, wouldn't Capel have welcomed her, drawing her into the musical society of the town?

Leyston was staring about him gloomily, his eyes disapproving. He went to peer at a calendar, printed in Czechoslovakia and showing a street scene in Brno. She had been too foreign . . . And perhaps that was the nub of it. Or had Shinglebourne proved too English?

'Let's go. I want to talk to Capel.'

Going out into the sun again was a relief, even though now it was wheeling low and preparing to slip into rising mist. Anglers were packing up and trailing over to their cars, but that was at the other end of the causeway. Here, the gulls had settled on the river, where they swam together as though holding a meeting.

He dropped Leyston at the police station and drove on alone to Capel's house. It was opposite the church, and three cars stood on the gravel sweep in front of it, beneath trees. Two had Doctor stickers; the third was Tanya Capel's Rover. He parked beside them and rang the bell. Capel himself opened the door.

'Come in, you old ruffian – I was afraid I was going to miss you!'

Capel was a man who would stand out anywhere: six foot

two, lean and angular, with a slanting forehead and a long straight nose. His bony hand gripped Gently's numbingly, and his eyes creased with pleasure.

'This is a social visit, of course.'

He had known Gently in a different capacity: three years before he had played a game of bluff with him that Gently had won; but it had left no rancour.

'I want to talk about an ex-patient.'

'I might have guessed you'd come on business.'

'Actually, I'm just lending a hand.'

'Look, come and say hallo to Tanya.'

Capel ushered him through to a drawing-room where Tanya Capel was seated beside a tea-tray. She rose smilingly to take Gently's hand, then began pouring out the cups.

'I thought you wouldn't be very long. Henry's been on pins since I gave him your message.'

'I was called out to a snotty-nosed kid,' Capel said. 'His parents thought he had measles, but it was only a rash. That's life as a sawbones.'

'I saw another car . . .'

'My son's. We've become partners now, you know. I've shovelled off all the old ladies on to him, and all the pregnancies I can duck out of.'

'He wants to meet your wife,' Tanya Capel smiled. 'And to tell the truth, so do I.'

It was almost bewildering, this social warmth, after the sad chillness of the dead woman's eyrie: two smiling people in a gracious room that during years had accepted the stamp of their personalities. The furniture was handsome but not new, ornaments had had time to settle into their groupings. In the background a gas fire, turned low, provided exactly the right touch of gentle comfort.

'Gabrielle is in France but she will be down next weekend.'

'Perhaps we could arrange – I don't know! Does your wife like music, old lad?'

'Music . . . ?'

'We could bring the quartet, which in point of fact is a quintet now. Leslie has taken up the clarinet, and even old Walt thinks he's rather good. So we could give you Walt's *Beach Suite* and *Festival Quintet*, and any amount of Mozart and Haydn. You've got a good room, have you?'

'Yes, but –!'

Gently had put at least one of that quartet through the mincer.

'If you think our cello will baulk, forget it. Leonard tends to regard you more as a benefactor. His wife went through with that divorce, and last year he made Laurel Mrs Meares.'

'Leonard is a different man,' Tanya Capel said. '*I* think the shake-up was just what he needed. But do say yes. It could be a housewarming, then we could meet your wife and talk our heads off.'

So it went on for twenty minutes, with cups emptied and recharged, until finally, with a long sigh, Capel said:

'What was that about an ex-patient . . . ?'

He took Gently to his den, a room crowded with bookcases and looking out through french windows to the big garden. Briefly, Gently explained what had happened; Capel listened with grave eyes.

'Hannah? Hannah Stoven?'

'Did you know her well?'

'Yes . . . sort of! Not *very* well, because nobody did. But heavens above . . . it's a bit of a shocker.' He folded his great frame into a chair. 'You couldn't be mistaken about the identity?'

'No.'

'But who would do such a thing?'

'Just before it, she had had intercourse.'

'Oh lord.'

Capel seemed much moved. He sat with arms dangling, gazing at nothing.

'According to her father, she was a fine violinist.'

'You have met him?'

'I meet everyone. He came to the Festival this year and had a chat with Walt and the rest of us. Hannah was with him. They worshipped each other. It'll be a terrible blow for him. Does he know?'

'He has been informed, but he's in Edinburgh on an engagement.'

'The poor devil, she was everything to him. Perhaps that was half the trouble.'

'What trouble?'

Capel shot him a look. 'Nobody else could get close to her. At least, that was my impression.'

'She came to you about her health?'

'Oh, that was nothing, just a cessation in her periods – I suppose I can talk about it now without infringing confidentiality. I asked her flat out if she'd had intercourse and after a bit she admitted it. But don't ask me who, that wasn't the question. A false alarm, I may say.'

'When was this?'

'In the spring. But I had known her long before that. I met her and her ex-husband when they first came down here and bought the tower. It's near the moorings. I pottered over to see what they were up to with it, then later on they bought the dinghy and became members of the club. I had a presentiment that they weren't happy together. I wasn't surprised to hear of the divorce.'

'What was he like?'

'A dried-up sort of fellow, with nothing in him except his job – an architect, you know. Once the tower was completed, he lost interest in it. Hannah was different. You felt she had enthusiasm, even passion, but as though it were blocked. Though with her father she was another person – they babbled Czech together like a couple of songbirds.'

'Would you describe her as friendly?'

'I suppose so. She took on the club accounts for us. She was trained as a book-keeper and worked part-time for Stan Claydon, our local bookseller. But you could never get near her. After I'd talked to her father I invited her to join us as a third violin, thinking it would get her into the swim and take her out of herself a bit. She just smiled in a distant sort of way and said she wasn't good enough for that, and nothing I could say would persuade her to have a go.' Capel studied his hands. 'Frankly, it amazed me to learn that she had a lover. I was eaten up with curiosity, but of course I couldn't ask her who it was.' He glanced at Gently. 'Is it him you're after?'

Gently stared back. 'Have you any suggestions?'

Capel rocked his shoulders. 'Not a suggestion exactly, just a shred of probably useless information. Two or three times when I've been sailing I've seen her dinghy moored at Harford, and always in the same place, alongside a black-painted yacht.'

'Do you know who owns it?'

Capel spread his hands. 'But I've seen the fellow sailing it. A fair-haired type, a bit of a dude. Sails with a plump lady who looks formidable.'

'What's the name of the yacht?'

'Ah. It's either *Jacqueline* or *Jacquinetta*.'

'Have you ever seen Mrs Stoven sailing with them?'

'No.'

'May I use your phone?'

'Help yourself.'

Leyston didn't know who the owner was either, but he promised to find out. And he had his own little titbit to add: according to the post office, the blurred postmark on the letter might also have originated at Harford.

'Could it be the same man?'

'That's possible. Dig him up as fast as you can.'

Gently hung up thoughtfully. A neat conjunction, but there could be no jumping to conclusions. Pottering around in her dinghy, Hannah Stoven might well have picked up an acquaintance with some innocent couple. But the handwriting? The nickname 'Chick'? Well, some time he'd track that down . . .

Capel, who'd sauntered down to stare through the window, now came back to his chair.

'Look here! I hope I haven't put the finger on some honest soul who barely knew her.'

Gently shrugged. 'We'll be discreet! Tell me about her acquaintance at the yacht club.'

'Well, I don't know.' Capel looked ruffled. 'With you, I can see I must watch my step. Actually, you could say I shaped like a suspect, because I've bought her a drink there myself. But so have Leonard and Tom Friday, not to mention the gallant Groupie.'

'Group Captain Riddlesworth?'

'You're on to him, are you? Then let me give you a small tip! Don't mention Lancasters to him. He flew in Halifaxes, and thinks that Lancs have stolen all the glamour.' Capel grimaced. 'He steers clear of me, but there's nothing personal in it. After all he must have gone through, he can't feel cheerful in the company of doctors.'

'What did he go through?'

'You've seen his face? It was half blown-off by a cannon-shell. All the same he brought his kite back, shot to bits, with the crew dead or dying. Decorated, of course. It was nearly a year before they managed to rebuild his face.'

'And he was friendly with Hannah . . . ?'

'I can see your nose twitching, but I'm pretty certain there was nothing in it. Perhaps just an exchange of mutual sympathy, since they were both casualties, in a sort of way. Injuries like Groupie's are traumatic. He has to live with a face that people stare at. Luckily he was married before it happened, so his life has been fairly normal that way – three children, two of them married, the youngest still a student. His wife is a neat-faced little woman, one hundred per cent officer's daughter.' Capel paused. 'Perhaps just because of that he would feel the abnormal side accentuated, that he was a man set aside by his face, a face that shocks and fails to express him. And behind that again his memories, recurrent nightmares that can't be shared.'

He massaged his bony hands and glanced sidelong at Gently. It was impossible to say if he felt sorry for Riddlesworth or was merely fascinated by him as a psychological type.

'And you regard Hannah as a casualty too?'

'A political victim, you could call her. She was twelve when her father defected and her life was torn up by the roots. Her mother was dead, she spoke no English, was alone with her father in a strange country. Stoven was around fifteen years older than her, and she probably chose him as a father-figure. But it didn't work out. In the end, it stayed her father and her, and self-chosen isolation.'

'Yet she was attractive.'

'Oh yes.'

Capel went on massaging his hands.

'Was Mrs Riddlesworth friendly with her?'

'I can't tell you that, because Sue Riddlesworth didn't frequent the club.'

'Riddlesworth bought Hannah drinks. What else?'

'I believe she sailed with him a couple of times – just Sunday afternoons on the river. Nothing you can read into that.'

'Had she sailed with other people?'

Capel shrugged. 'Anyway, it happened last summer.'

'You never saw them together except at the club?'

Capel merely spread his hands.

And probably in fact it had gone no further: simply two lonely people recognising each other. In a distant way, kindred spirits, but the way too distant to admit of development.

'And he was her only special friend.'

'I'm not sure I would put it even so high. No doubt if you ask him he will tell you much the same things about me. I tried to chat her up too, and to inveigle her into my clutches.' Capel grinned. 'Luckily, I have an alibi. Alibis are one thing a doctor is flush with.'

'What about this bookseller, her employer?'

'I've seen her out with him on one occasion. That was at the White Hart, during this year's Festival, when she was waiting for her father. Stan was dining there, and joined her in the bar, doubtless to discuss some matter of business.'

'Is he married?'

'Oh, dear! Stan really is a most unlikely customer. He's a

little spectacled man, about fifty, always worried about his business. Haven't you talked to him?'

'Not yet.'

'He's a client, so I ought not to be discussing him. Yes, he's married, and his wife is an invalid who has a housekeeper-companion to look after her.' Capel sighed. 'Just between ourselves, she's one of the patients I've unloaded on Leslie.'

'An imaginary invalid?'

Capel touched his large nose. 'That has to remain between me and Hippocrates.'

Was he really making progress, or merely going through the routine of stopping earths? The more Gently probed the imaginable prospects, the more improbable they seemed to get. Yet someone, somewhere, had pierced the reserve that Hannah Stoven had cast about herself: as early as that spring she had been worried enough to come to Capel for a test. And yesterday . . . by land or by water . . . that someone had joined her again: she had gone to meet him, he hadn't come to the tower: he was obviously a secret that must be kept.

Because of his reputation, or hers?

Or just because her reserve insisted on complete discretion?

The doorbell rang, and Capel was instantly on the alert. But a moment later it was Leyston's long face that peered round the door.

'If I could speak to you . . . sir.'

Gently rose.

'Shall we be seeing you again?' Capel asked. 'How about a bite later on? Then I could introduce you to Leslie.'

'I can't promise.'

'Give me a ring if you like the idea of a spot of music.'

He accompanied them to the door, and winked at Gently behind Leyston's back. Old Mutton-chops! At a window, Tanya Capel waved a goodbye.

They got into Gently's car.

'Harford have identified the yacht,' Leyston said. 'The *Jacquetta*. It's the only black yacht that moors at Harford. It belongs to the husband of a local licensee.'

'The husband?'

'She owns the Eel's Foot. It's a free house with a bit of a restaurant. The people's name is Shavers.'

'Shavers! Are you sure of that?'

Leyston chose to look offended.

'Is it a Donald Shavers?'

'Harford didn't say. He was out when I rang. His wife said he was probably at the boatyard putting the winter cover on his boat.'

Shavers: it was the name Gently had been angling for ever since he had seen the note from the handbag. Donald 'Chick' Shavers was a minor villain who had come his way five years before. There had been a shooting in an Acton warehouse used by a cannabis-smuggling ring, as a result of which Narcotics had swooped and cleaned up the whole operation. Shavers had been a suspect for the shooting, but had come off with three years on a handling charge. Fair-haired and a bit of a dude: yes, that described Donald 'Chick' Shavers. And he had covered sheets of statement paper with that identical, swaggering handwriting . . .

A convicted dope-handler, owner of a yacht, residing in a village on the coast: whether or not he was concerned with Hannah Stoven, 'Chick' Shavers still deserved a little attention!

'Has he any form here?'

'Any form?'

Not bothering to answer, Gently started his engine. One way or another, he felt that his day wasn't going to be wasted.

3

Mist was rising from the river again when they drove over the bridge at Thwaite, and the narrow stream they had left there had grown to a flood that covered the mud shoals. Just past the Maltings, through a fringe of trees, one glimpsed the windows of a house, and at gates to a drive a stocky, blazered figure stood watching the car go by.

Beside Gently, Leyston stirred.

'How well do you think that man really knew her?'

Gently drove on a little further before grunting:

'I doubt if she was soaking him, if that's the idea.'

'I've met his wife and she could be a tartar. He wouldn't want her to get wind of a fancy piece. Then he's a big man on committees and fund-raising stunts, as well as chief sponsor of the concert hall. In a scandal, he'd have plenty to lose.'

Gently shook his head. 'It doesn't fit.'

Meaning that it didn't fit the picture of Hannah Stoven which was slowly taking shape in his mind. Essentially she was a secret person, probably living an intense hidden life: a life that bubbled over only with one other person, the father whom she saw but at intervals. And probably it was a father-image she had seen in Riddlesworth, rather than that of a lover. A vital person with, deep in her shell, a yearning tenderness: a blocked passion.

'She had a bit of money put away,' Leyston mused.

But those few thousands weren't enough. They could have been presents from her father, or simple savings, since she didn't run a car and the tower was costing her no rent. No: if Riddlesworth was the culprit then the motive was more obscure. She would have shrunk from revealing such a secret, even if willing to put the bite on him . . .

'What's the name of this forest?'

For a while now the road had been running by plantations of pine, spoked by twilit rides and skirted by fiery beeches and maples. The massed trees were quite dark, suggesting that the sections ran deep. Bracken that was russet along the verges showed yellow and green below the pines.

'Foulden Forest. It's quite big.'

For a mile or more they kept in touch with it, but finally the road bore away seawards and shortly they were entering a large village.

'Harford . . .'

They drove into a square, closed at one end by a church, at the other by trees above which rose the castellations of a lofty keep. Two or three shops and a couple of pubs were dotted among picturesque houses, while the centre of the square offered parking. There a uniformed man was waiting.

'P.C. Sutton. Your man isn't back yet, but I can show you where he keeps his boat.'

In speaking, he had glanced towards one of the pubs, which stood a little back, with metal tables in front of it. In its doorway stood a stout, dark-haired woman, hands on hips, scowling at them. Quite unabashed, she continued to stare, and had the appearance of defying them to walk over.

'Is that Mrs Shavers?'

'Yes sir. She was none too pleased to have me calling.'

'Have you had any problems with the Shavers?'

'No sir. They keep a quiet house.'

And there stood the reason!

'Get in.'

Sutton pointed out the road. It dropped down from the level of the square to pass by cottages and some derelict maltings. Then, surmounting a flood-baulk, they came to the river, which here was much wider than at Thwaite or Shinglebourne, and widened still further on the downstream reach to provide buoyed moorings for a number of craft. Straight ahead was a short jetty equipped with some manner of lifting gear, and upstream a beach where small boats were pulled up, along with one or two stored yachts.

37

'How far is the sea from here?'

'As the crow flies, a couple of hundred yards, sir.'

'And downstream?'

'Another six miles. That's where the spit ends, at Shingle Point.'

In fact, down there at the jetty, the sea might have been a hundred miles away. The spit, with a covering of coarse marsh vegetation, was just high enough to conceal it from view. Upstream and down stretched dour marshes which everywhere were steaming under mist, while the moored boats, streamed on the flood, each presented a stern to the jetty.

'A quiet spot like this . . . don't you get any smuggling?'

'I daresay there was some in the old days, sir. But nothing lately.'

'Do you get foreign yachts here?'

'Once in a while you'll see a Dutchman.'

Sutton led them along the bank between tarred store-sheds and the pulled-up boats. They had to step over sleepers and wend round timber, oil drums and frames hung with nets. The bank seemed deserted: doubtless those who normally frequented it were at home, tuned in to the football.

'That'll be him, sir.'

At the very top end a black-painted yacht stood supported by oil drums, partly hidden by a canvas cover drawn along it as far as the well. Puddles lay around it, and its bilges were still damp from scrubbing. On other oil drums lay the mast in a raffle of wire shrouds.

Nobody seemed in attendance, but from inside came sounds of scrubbing. Gently tapped on the hull:

'Chick . . . ?'

A moment later, a face was staring down at them.

'Well, well!'

For a brief instant, fear had flickered in the man's eyes, as they went first to Gently, then to Leyston, then to the uniformed Sutton. But he quickly got control of himself. He came out a bit further from under the cover.

'So what do you know! I thought it was a mate of mine, then I look out to see a deputation. You and all, Chiefie. Has someone nicked the crown jewels?'

'Are you surprised to see me, Chick?'

'Surprised – I'm flabbergasted.'

'So come down here where I can talk to you.'

'Well – as long as it isn't a bust.'

He hung on for a few seconds, his eyes switching again to Leyston and Sutton; then, shrugging, he clambered out of the well and down a short ladder. He was wearing a boiler suit, and some of the grime from his hands had got on his face. About forty, he had small, close-set eyes, marring otherwise personable features. He wasn't, as Gently knew, a common villain, but came from a respectable East End background, his father being the chief buyer for a firm of fruit-importers. But Donald Shavers had turned out shiftless and with little interest in regular work. For a while he had lived on the earnings of women, then had graduated into the rackets.

Now he stood warily at the foot of the ladder, facing them with an expression of careful innocence.

'Is this your yacht, Chick?'

'What if it is?'

'When did you haul it out?'

'I hauled out this morning, if you want to know. But what's that got to do with you lot?'

'Then yesterday you were on moorings.'

'Suppose I was. That's my buoy, over there.'

'And you were on board?'

'Yes, I'm telling you, I was getting the gear off her.'

'And that's your dinghy – with the outboard?'

Shavers' eyes were getting more and more cautious. Involuntarily he was wiping his hands on the overalls which, in spite of some soiling, looked freshly-laundered.

'Look – what's this about? Here I am, minding my own sodding business, then away come you three blokes and start asking questions like I was on a caper. What am I supposed to have done?'

'Don't you know, Chick?'

'Do me a favour. What should I have done?'

'Yesterday, at what time were you on your yacht?'

'All the afternoon – just ask someone.'

'You're claiming an alibi for the afternoon?'

'Yes – no! I don't need any alibi. Anyway, in the morning I was at home, I was serving in the bar till after two.'

'You were alone on the yacht?'

'There were blokes about here . . . ask around, they'll soon tell you.'

'Moored to that buoy, the furthest upstream?'

'So what?'

'With the use of an outboard dinghy?'

Shavers' mouth hung open slightly and his uneasy eyes flitted to Sutton. Yet still the uneasiness was struggling with indignation and a sort of bafflement that might well have been genuine. He passed a grubby hand over his pale hair.

'So some geezer was croaked – is that it?'

'Is it?'

'Yes, it is – or why would they have called in a nob like you? You aren't Narcotics, and everyone knows I'm out of that caper for good. So someone's been done, and here I am, a poor bleeder with a record – and straightaway you jump on me, who's been going straight ever since I got out! Ask him.' He gestured to Sutton. 'I'll bet he never even knew I had a record.'

Sutton, a heavy-faced man, looked a little pink; but said nothing.

'So you're out of the business.'

'Listen, Chiefie, I've done my time and I'm on the level.'

'You're just living down here because you like the place. Along with your yacht. And your outboard dinghy.'

'Sod my outboard dinghy! Why shouldn't I live here?'

'You never did tell us where the stuff came in.'

'Because I never knew . . .'

Gently stared hard at him. 'Then you won't mind if we take out a warrant for the Eel's Foot.'

'Oh, bloody hel.'

Now it was bafflement that had got the upper hand. Shavers stood working his hands and scowling at the puddles under the yacht. Near him stood a bucket of filthy water and a long-handled scrubbing brush; in sudden exasperation he grabbed the bucket and emptied it towards the river.

'I'm up the effing creek, aren't I?'

'Let's have the truth about where you were yesterday.'

'But I've told you. And if someone's been done, I don't know the first thing about it.'

'So why the alibi for the afternoon?'

'It wasn't a bloody alibi! You came asking me, didn't you? And I told you. How did I know I needed an alibi?'

'That's what I'd like to know.'

'If I'd wanted an alibi, I could have thought up a better tale than that.'

'So start thinking.'

'But what have I done?'

'Perhaps we should begin at the Eel's Foot.'

Shavers pitched the bucket under the yacht and gave it a kick for good measure. The frustration in his face was comical, and twice he seemed about to blurt something out. At last he turned to Gently.

'Look, Chiefie, you and me speak the same language! I'm in a bind, I have to admit it, but I could tell you some things you'd like to hear. So why don't we have a quiet chat, just you and me together? You're from the Smoke, so you'll understand . . . there are things a bloke doesn't want blabbed out.'

'You have something to confess?'

'No! Just personal like, that's all.'

A whining note had come into his voice and the small eyes were fixed on Gently's pleadingly.

Gently glanced at Leyston's face of stone, and at the restive figure of Sutton. Once more, he was going to steal the local man's thunder, and this time in front of a subordinate . . . But there was nothing else for it.

'All right. I'll listen to you.'

'Chiefie, I swear you won't regret it!'

'We'll talk on the yacht.' Impassively, Gently turned to Leyston. 'Perhaps you'll wait for me at the car.'

Shavers replaced floorboards that had been set to air and hung a portable gas lantern over the chart-table, but that was the extent of the comfort to be found in the womb of the stripped-out yacht. The cabin reeked with moisture and condensation fuzzed the metal frames and glass of the opened portholes; to sit on there were only the bare bunk-boards, much too low and with no backrests.

Properly, it was only a single-cabined boat, though a spare bunk forward was tucked deep into the forepeak. Opposite it was the toilet, and at the aft end of the cabin quarter-bunks vanished under the galley and chart-table. But now it was all damp woodwork with a dulled sweet smell of varnish and bilge.

Having lit the lamp, Shavers squatted and turned earnest eyes on Gently.

'Chiefie, you've got to believe this – I've got nothing on my conscience!'

Gently stared at him before grunting: 'Is that all you've got to say?'

'No – I'm going to tell you, aren't I? But you've got to look at my position. Those other two wouldn't understand, while you, you know the whole story.'

'I know you did three years for handling cannabis, and one for living on immoral earnings.'

'That's just it, it's all behind me – an ex-con can go straight, can't he? And now I'm all fixed up with Myrtle – a couple of years, and no trouble. I run the bar, I've got this little boat, and nobody here knows a thing. Not except Myrtle, that is. She knows I've had my bit of bother.'

Gently hunched. One had heard this before! And once in a blue moon it might be true. Smudge-faced, his hair tousled, Shavers continued to eye him imploringly.

'Where does Myrtle come into it?'

'You see? A man like you can put things together. I've done

my time, so I can tell you now . . . as long as you don't put it about who grassed. You're thinking we brought the dope in here – well, you're right. This was the pick-up. The stuff came over from Holland once a month on a big ketch-rigged Dutch yacht. She dropped her hook off the spit and ferried it to the beach in a dinghy, and it was my job to be waiting over there with a suitcaseful of cash. Then back I'd come across the river and deliver the stuff to a car waiting on the jetty – and then away it went to the Smoke for the lads to parcel it up. And yes – you're right again – I'd be staying up at Myrtle's. That's how I got to know her, spending a couple of nights there once a month.'

'Didn't she know what your game was?'

'Chiefie, she's straight as the Bank of England. She stood by me all the same, never missing a visit when I was in Brixton.' He jerked up suddenly. 'Stone the crows! You didn't go looking for me there, did you?'

'P.C. Sutton enquired for you.'

'Sod my luck. I'll have to think up some story . . .'

His eyes for a moment were panicky, and then his mouth twisted.

'I daresay you're getting the idea now! It's true, Myrtle watches me like a hawk. The least little bit of bother, and –' He drew his hand across his throat.

'Is she as tough as all that?'

'I'm telling you. I just have to keep my nose clean, Chiefie.'

'You are her husband, I take it?'

For answer, Shavers got up to squint through a porthole.

'No need for that stupid bobby to know, but Myrtle just took my name . . . I'm on trial, you might say. That's what I've been trying to tell you, Chiefie.'

He slumped back on the bunk, and sat staring unhappily at his knees. Like the woodwork, his forehead was beginning to gleam, and one could hear his quick breathing in the close silence of the yacht.

'And this is the *only* reason why you don't want us to search the Eel's Foot?'

'I swear it, Chiefie. You go in there, and I'll be out on my ear before you can spit.'

'Yet here you are. With your yacht and dinghy.'

'But I keep telling you, that game is over! Now would I have let on what I did if I was still picking up the goods?'

'What's the name of the ketch?'

Shavers gulped. 'It's the *Seven Seas*, from Scheveningen. But don't go putting it about –'

'What's the captain's name?'

'Hans Kloostermans.'

'And you're positive you have nothing on your conscience?'

'No . . .'

'Nothing you wouldn't let on to Myrtle?'

'What are you getting at?'

'I've just been reading a letter of yours, making a rendezvous with a girl friend.'

Shavers stared wide-eyed, his mouth drooping. Then he hugged himself, and groaned.

Gently lit his pipe with deliberation, sending clouds of grey smoke round the yacht's sweating cabin. In spite of the lantern it was chill in there, as though a frost had come on with the mist and the darkness. Outside there was no sound. He smoked with slow, measured puffs. For some moments, Shavers watched him with wretched eyes, slumped a little, his mouth small.

'Tell me straight, Chiefie . . . she's dead, isn't she?'

'Is she?'

'She's got to be! It's the chop when they call you in, not sodding dope. You were having me on.'

'Where were you yesterday afternoon?'

'I've told you, and I'll tell you again –'

'You were out in your dinghy.'

'But I never was! I was on board, stripping out.'

'So nobody could have seen you upstream.'

'If they say they did, they're liars.'

'They couldn't have seen you at Shinglebourne.'

'No they couldn't.'

'Or near Thwaite.'

Shavers' mouth set tight.

'All the same, you admit that Hannah Stoven was your girl friend.'

'I'm admitting sod all.'

'We've got your letter. She received it yesterday.'

'Don't talk stupid – that was last week!'

'So you knew her. You wrote her letters, and she used to visit you on this yacht. She has been here, in this cabin, sitting, lying on one of these berths.'

'Oh, sod it. Sod everything!'

'We have a witness who saw her here. And I can see how she might have become inconvenient when you were working a meal-ticket like Myrtle.'

Shavers bored at a bunk-board with his fist, his grimy face working tormentedly. Unmoved, Gently went on puffing, peering at Shavers through wreaths of smoke.

'She could have tried to screw you.'

'It wasn't like that!'

'So tell me how it was.'

'You'd only laugh . . . a man like me and a peach of a skirt like Hannah.'

'Why would I laugh?'

'Because . . .'

'Let's start at the beginning. How did you meet her?'

It was grotesque: you got the feeling that Shavers was on the point of bursting into tears. He was hugging himself, turned away from the lamp, a lock of hair fallen over his face.

'Her engine conked out. That's how I met her.'

'Go on.'

'Well, that's how it was. One day when I was on board. I got out the dinghy and towed her in.'

'When did this happen?'

'Last June some time.'

'You're sure it wasn't earlier?'

'It was just after my birthday, and that's June 22nd.'

Gently blew a ring. 'She came on board.'

'Yes, but it isn't what you think! She wasn't that sort, Hannah wasn't, and I didn't haul her on to a bunk. She'd got class, you understand? I don't know how to tell you . . . She was a foreigner, for one thing. She'd got a funny way of talking.'

'Just your style.'

'Listen, Chiefie, I know my way about too! I've had women from here till breakfast, I thought I could make the grade with a duchess. But Hannah was different somehow . . . more like a sister. Like that.'

'And you never touched her.'

'We just . . . talked.'

'She kept coming back – and you just talked.'

'So bleeding laugh, I don't care. But I never laid a finger on her. You could talk to her, tell her things, more than any skirt I've ever met. I told her what sort of villain I was and it never set her against me. I told her about Myrtle, about the pub. Somehow you felt she'd understand.'

'Wasn't it dangerous to open up like that?'

Shavers shook his head impatiently. He was staring at the cabin-sole, not at Gently, and kneading his hands between his knees.

'Hannah was all right. She didn't come often, just on the bottom of the ebb. Then she'd take the flood back. When the tide was wrong, she went the other way.'

'Didn't you meet her up there?'

'No. Nor I didn't go to her place, either. It was always on the yacht. That's what she wanted, and that's the way it was. I tell you, she was more like a sister, someone you could talk to who wasn't against you. There was something special about Hannah . . . I can't put it into words.'

'Did you mention her to Myrtle?'

'Do me a favour. Why should I cut my own throat?'

'Did she never find out?'

'No she didn't. She's used to me sodding off to the yacht. Up there on the mooring is out of the way, I'm the last buoy upriver. Some of the lads round here might have spotted it, but they wouldn't have shopped me to Myrtle.'

'So what about the letter?'

'I tell you, that was last week, when I wasn't sure I could make it.' He dragged on his hands. 'I didn't know then that it was going to be the last time I'd see her.'

'It was the last time?'

'Bloody yes.'

'Nobody could have seen her with you yesterday.'

'Look, Chiefie, the sodding tide was wrong – it had started running up by half-past two.'

'Which would have taken you upstream.'

He rocked his shoulders. 'Can't I get you to understand? If I'd gone up to Shinglebourne on the top of the tide, it would have taken me four hours to get back. That bleeding dinghy isn't a speedboat, and I was back at the pub by five.'

'But you have a car, don't you?'

His eyes were wary. 'What's my car got to do with it?'

'Tides don't bother a car, and there's a place where the road runs close to the river.'

'So what about that?'

But fear was back; you could smell it in the smoke-filled cabin. Gently took a few puffs off, his eye considering Shavers.

'Did you have your car out?'

'Well – yes. I was getting my gear out, wasn't I?'

'So then you could have made a little trip. Like down the back road by Bodney church.'

'What are you getting at?'

'Didn't you?'

'So help me, I never did.'

'To the place where you can get down to the bank – where there's deep water and a pull-up?'

'But I didn't!'

'Still, you know where I mean.'

'Why shouldn't I know –'

'You didn't meet her there?'

'Christ, no.' Shavers stared, his jaw slowly dropping. 'Is that where . . . ?'

47

Gently went on puffing. Shaver's eyes had a stunned look. He swallowed several times, his dirty hands clasped tight.

'How . . . ?'

Gently said nothing.

'But why? Why her?'

'Perhaps she was in someone's way.'

'Not Hannah – not her.'

'If she knew too much . . .'

Shavers still looked shocked. 'It's just bleeding unfair, that's all! There's others that no bastard would miss . . . but Hannah. Who'd play a sodding trick like that?'

Was he acting? On a previous occasion he had been through Gently's hands, and then he had proved a facile liar, but never bright enough to make it stick. And the line he was taking was unexpected: Gently found himself unable to make up his mind.

'You say she just came to talk?'

'I swear it!'

'Then she would have talked about herself.'

'Well, a bit, she did. But you know me – it was mostly me talking and her listening.'

'Did she mention any men?'

'She wasn't that sort –'

'Did she name any man to you?'

Shavers stared for a while. 'Like the man she worked for, and her dad. And a bloke at the yacht club.'

'Which one?'

'She didn't say his name. Just that he'd taken her out in his boat . . . could that shit have done it?'

'Who else?'

'Another bloke at the club. A doctor.'

Gently sighed to himself.

'Now listen, Chick. When you said you were up the creek you were right. You knew the victim, you had opportunity, and I can think of a couple of fat motives. So if you're innocent you'd better speak up and tell me anything else you know. Because if you don't, it's ten to one that Inspector Leyston will be feeling your collar.'

'But for chrissake, Chiefie, I don't know anything! If I did, I'd bloody tell you. I want you to catch the bastard too. If I knew who it was, I'd kick his head in.'

'Just bear it in mind, that's all.'

Shavers gulped. 'Are you taking me in?'

Gently stared and blew smoke-rings for several moments, then shook his head. 'Just stay around.'

'You believe me, Chiefie!'

'I believe nothing.'

'And you aren't going to queer me up with Myrtle?'

Gently shrugged, and got to his feet.

'Try to think up a good tale to tell her . . .'

Outside the dark and the mist combined to make the bank an awkward obstacle course. Sutton sat waiting in the car with Leyston; getting in, it was to the former that Gently turned.

'How long have you been stationed at Harford?'

'Just on two years, sir.'

'Five years ago they were running cannabis in here. The ring was broken up. Shavers was one of them; he's done his time, and for all I know he's going straight. For your information, the stuff came from Scheveningen in a ketch called *Seven Seas*, captain Hans Kloostermans.'

'You want an eye kept on Shavers, sir?'

'Just bringing you up to date. I doubt if there is anything going on now, but if you spot a Dutchman, report at once.'

Leyston said dully: 'Do we take Shavers with us?'

'We shall need witnesses to break his story.'

Leyston made no comment. He was smoking a cigarette and staring ahead into the mist.

Down there, when Gently switched on his lights, the visibility was barely twenty yards.

4

Away from the river the mist was less dense, except for occasional swirling patches, and along the fringe of the forest the pallid maples stepped out like a succession of looming ghosts. At the Maltings it was thick again, with a fuzz of light denoting a pub that neighboured the bridge; then they lost it altogether when the road struck higher ground towards the town.

As he drove, Gently gave Leyston a synopsis of the interview with Shavers. The local man listened silently, at most interjecting a curt monosyllable. Well – perhaps Gently would have felt the same! Yet if Leyston had sat in, Shavers would never have opened up; while if he had handed over to the sad-faced Inspector Shavers might have buttoned his lip entirely. To a certain extent Shavers had been right: he and Gently spoke the same language. They knew the game . . . and perhaps it was this, most of all, that was offending poor Leyston.

At the station Leyston's sergeant, Mason, waited with the results of the search of the river bank. All they had found was a spot among the gorses where apparently two people were in the habit of lying down.

'The grass was flattened . . . I'd say the spot had been used pretty often. There were patches of bare earth as though they might have put down a ground-sheet.'

'How far into the bushes?'

'Not far, but you have to push between bushes to get to it.'

So over a period, perhaps all summer, there had been rendezvous at that secret place, with Hannah, or her lover, coming prepared for damp grass. Perhaps Shavers had told the truth, and her visits to him had been quite innocent – because wasn't he another lame duck, like the Group Captain, with whom she might have found a tenuous compatibility? No need for him, if she had been his mistress, to go carting ground-sheets into the gorses: also there had been another point about which he could have seen no reason to lie.

'May I use your phone?'

Capel answered the phone as though he'd been waiting for it to ring.

'Listen . . . I would like to know the exact date when you saw Mrs Stoven.'

'Half a mo till I find her card . . . it was the twenty-second of May. I made a test, and she called in the next day for the result.'

'Thanks.'

'I say, are you joining us for a meal?'

'Sorry, but I doubt if I shall be through.'

He hung up, and met Leyston's resentful eye.

'About Shavers. One small problem.'

'A problem . . . ?'

'He says he met Stoven first at the end of June, but it was May twenty-second when she went for a pregnancy test.'

Leyston looked down his nose.

'So if he's telling the truth . . .'

'There must have been another man, since May at least.'

Leyston stared blankly: perhaps he thought Gently was going to produce him out of a bag.

'Shavers is an ex-con.'

'I doubt if he was lying.'

'But all the same . . . if there was another man, Shavers might have got to know and caught them at it, and finished her off in a row.'

'Yes – he might.'

But did it square, either with Shavers' character or hers? Shavers was vulnerable and he was no fool: he wouldn't easily be tempted to step out of line. While Hannah, for her part, would probably never even have hinted to him that she had another interest.

'To get him, we'll have to break his alibi, but the other man is our top priority. Have you talked to her employer?'

'Not yet.'

'Let's see if he can fill us in.'

Leyston sniffed, and rose reluctantly; clearly, he was liking the idea of Shavers.

Considering the modest size of the town, Claydon's Bookshop was ambitious; it had three large windows to the street and combined the sale of books with fancy goods. One entered a spacious, well-lit store that smelled of paper and printing ink, with access on one side to the fancy goods section and on the other to a secondhand book department. Girls in pastel overalls manned the counters, where a few late customers still lingered. The book stock was large and looked intelligently arranged, though here and there bookshelves showed gaps.

'Where is Mr Claydon?'

'He's in the office.'

The girl behind the counter was pretty and smiling. She threw a curious look at Leyston, whom no doubt she recognised.

'When do you close?'

'Well, we're closed now, actually . . .'

'I would be obliged if the staff stayed behind for a few minutes. Just to answer a couple of questions.'

Her smile faded slightly. 'I'll tell the others . . .'

They went through into a stock-room, in the corner of which was a minute office. It was barely large enough to contain the desk, typist's table and filing-cabinets with which it was cluttered. At the desk a small, spare man in black-framed glasses sat squinting at an open analysis-book. Other account books were ranged around him, and a cigarette burned on an ashtray at his elbow.

'Mr Claydon?'

The man started and gazed up at him. Behind the glasses, his eyes looked huge.

'Yes? What is it?'

Gently introduced himself and inserted his bulky frame into the office.

'What is it you want?' Claydon's stare was unfriendly.

'We are making enquiries about one of your employees.'

'Who? What employee?'

'Mrs Stoven.'

'Her!'

'We would like to know what you can tell us about her.'

Claydon's mouth opened a little to show small, nicotine-stained teeth. He grabbed nervously for the cigarette and inhaled some quick puffs.

'What has she been up to?'

'Have you heard no news about her?'

'News . . . ? What should I have heard?'

'Perhaps you should prepare yourself for a shock, Mr Claydon. Mrs Stoven has met with an accident.'

'An accident!'

'When did you last see her?'

Claydon puffed hard on the cigarette. The hand holding it was trembling, and he was squinting as though the smoke were stinging his eyes.

'Are you telling me she's dead?'

'I'm afraid so.'

'Oh my God. How – how did it happen?'

'We'll come to that. When was she last here?'

'Yesterday. Yesterday morning she got out the wages.'

'Did she mention any plans for the afternoon?'

'Wait . . . she said she was going out in her boat.'

He was plainly shaken. The cigarette kept bobbing, and his eyes weren't seeing Gently. His sallow, rather foxy face had gone a shade paler.

'Was it . . . drowning?'

The words seemed forced from him.

'Mrs Stoven was attacked.'

'Oh no. Who did it?'

'We are hoping you may be able to help us.'

He stubbed out the cigarette, but then at once lit another; already, the ashtray was overflowing with a score or more of stubs. His fingers were deeply stained and the squint seemed a permanent habit. After a number of heavy drags, he gestured shakily to the account books.

'This couldn't have happened at a worse time. *I* don't know what she's been up to. And now, if it's as you say . . . well, it's just one disaster after another . . .'

'She kept your books?'

He nodded. 'It was my accountant who suggested her. She went to him for a job, but he didn't have a vacancy. So I took her on, one day and two mornings a week, keeping the books, paying accounts, working out the wages and handling the mail. She could do it, she was trained. I raised her money a couple of times. But I thought I ought to keep in touch with the books . . . this afternoon, I've been going through them.'

'Is there a discrepancy?'

'It's double dutch! Look, can you figure out this writing?'

He pointed to the column headings in the analysis-book, abbreviations scribbled in a spidery hand.

'I can work out some of it from the figures, but most of it is a mystery – and now what the devil am I going to do? Only, one thing is wretchedly plain.'

He took more drags, his eyes watering.

'Do you suspect Mrs Stoven of embezzlement?'

'No, not that . . . I don't see how it's possible. The cash she handled always checked, and of course the cheques she made out I signed myself. No, Hannah was honest, I'll swear to that, but how am I ever to sort this lot out? And that's not the worst of it . . . she's allowed the VAT to run, and never thought to warn me.'

'Could that be serious?'

The cigarette bobbled. 'I've got to pay it by the end of the month. If I don't, I'll have them in here . . . somewhere, I've got to find it up.'

'Is it for much?'

'On fancy goods and stationery . . . it's more than I know how to lay my hands on.'

He sat staring miserably at the spread-out books, looking not unlike an elderly schoolboy. A slight figure, he was clad in a charcoal pinstripe, with a black bow tie dragged a little awry.

'How well did you know Mrs Stoven?'

54

'Meaning . . . what?'

'Did you know her before she became an employee?'

'Oh, yes.' He gulped smoke. 'I knew her when she was still married. She and her husband were customers, he used to come hunting for architecture books. She wanted me to order her books in Czech – I suppose you know who her father is.'

'What sort of man was her husband?'

'Clever, I should think, but I never paid him much attention.' He gave Gently a wavery look. 'Why do you ask?'

Gently stared back without answering.

'When she came to work here, you'd get to know her better.'

'Naturally one gets to know one's staff.'

'I'm told she was a friendly person.'

'Otherwise, I wouldn't have engaged her.'

'She would have worked in here?'

'Of course. That's her table there, with her things in the drawer.'

'If I may, I'll take a look.'

'You may. But she kept nothing personal here.'

He had to get up and move his chair to enable Gently to squeeze by him to the table. The drawer contained only ballpens, a ruler, some cigarettes and a book of matches. The two latter were of the same brands as those found in her handbag.

Claydon gazed at them, his mouth twitching.

'Yesterday, she offered me one of those . . .'

'You had grown fond of Hannah.'

'Yes . . . I'll admit it. Though I can't forgive her the hole she's got me into.'

'Mrs Stoven was strangled.'

'Oh, heavens.'

'Did she ever mention a boy friend to you?'

'No . . . never . . .'

'Did she speak of any friends?'

'Forgive me . . . I'm not feeling so well.'

He dropped down on his chair, leaving Gently stranded in the small space at the back of the office. After a shrug, Gently pulled out the typist's chair and sat. Claydon looked as though he might be sick. He was leaning over the desk with stopped breathing. From the direction of the curtain that hid the shop, one could hear excited whispering, then a giggle.

'I'm sorry . . . I suppose it's the shock . . . that and the mess I'm in, anyway. Yesterday she was as well as you or I. She was talking about taking the tide upriver . . .'

'Did she say she was meeting someone?'

'I don't remember.'

'Hannah Stoven had a lover.'

Claydon gaped.

'Yesterday she kept a rendezvous with a man, near Bodney church.'

'I – I can scarcely believe that.'

'Take it as true. She had had a lover for at least the past six months. Perhaps someone living in the Thwaite direction, or possibly at Harford. I want you to think very carefully of any names she may have dropped.'

'But . . . she didn't seem to have many friends.'

'Think. During all the time she was working here.'

Claydon was very pale, and his cigarette burned unnoticed between his fingers. He sat frowning through the heavy-framed glasses, supported by an elbow on the desk.

'At Thwaite, she knew Group Captain Riddlesworth.'

'She told you that?'

'I know she used to go sailing with him. But that was last year . . . wait! I remember his name coming up again, yesterday.'

'In what connection?'

Claydon noticed the cigarette and took a few, fluttery drags.

'It was about a book he had on order . . . a history of Bomber Command. She said that if she saw him, she'd let him know it had come in.'

'If she saw him?'

'I suppose she thought she would be going in his direction, I don't know! But that's what she said. Only I can't think the Group Captain . . .'

'Have you ever seen them together?'

'No – well, only once here in the shop. She went to check a title in the secondhand stock, and he was there, and they chatted a moment.'

'Did his manner seem familiar?'

'Just friendly. They seemed pleased to see each other.'

'When was this?'

'One day recently. I can't remember which.'

He buried his second cigarette in the ashtray, then glanced towards the packet, but didn't light another. Meanwhile the curtain had twitched once or twice, though now there was silence in that direction.

'I think the staff want to go . . .'

'Call them in.'

Claydon hesitated, then did as he was bid. Four girls, now divested of overalls, came to cluster round the office door. Rather waspishly, Claydon introduced them. The pretty girl was his senior, a Miss Burton. Though they probably couldn't have heard what was passing in the office, they had a serious air as they faced Gently.

'Which of you knew Hannah Stoven well?'

They looked at each other, at a loss. At last Miss Burton ventured:

'Once she took me out in her boat.'

'When was that?'

'Oh . . . in the summer. In August, I think it was.'

'Was there any special reason?'

'I was at a loose end . . . I suppose she knew it, and asked me out.'

'Which way did you go?'

'It had to be downstream, because that's how the tides were. Hannah said she knew a man at Harford and we moored up there, but we didn't meet him. She said he must be sailing further down.'

'Did she mention his name?'

'No.'

'What did you talk about on the trip?'

Miss Burton was getting a little warm. She was a plumpish girl with fluffy light brown hair and an appealing mouth.

'Well . . . the usual thing! I'd had a row with my boy, and he'd cleared off with friends for the weekend. I suppose I was full of that. Hannah knew I'd been having problems.'

'You talked about boy friends?'

'More or less. We talked about all sorts of things.'

'She told you she had a boy friend?'

'Yes, and that surprised me quite a bit.'

'Did she tell you his name?'

· 'No. But she had a sort of dreamy look when she talked about him. She said he didn't live in the town and that he was nobody I would know. She said he was interested in music, like her, and that it was all very romantic, but that it couldn't last, and for his sake she would have to break it off.'

'Because he was married?'

Miss Burton dimpled. 'She didn't say that in so many words! And I didn't know whether to believe her or not, she talked in such a queer way.'

'How was it queer?'

'It's hard to explain. As though she were talking about a dream, her eyes sort of in the distance. I was pretty sure she was making it up.'

'Had you ever seen her in the company of a man?'

'Oh no.'

Gently glanced round the little group.

'Anyone?'

A tall girl with glasses said: 'It probably doesn't count, but once or twice I've seen her with Group Captain Riddlesworth.'

'You've seen them where?'

'Oh, at the yacht club, where my father is a member. And once going towards the Martello Tower. Though I couldn't say if she invited him in.'

Gently regarded the little group sternly.

'As you may have guessed, something rather serious has happened. It is important that the police should know about any men friends Hannah had. Can anyone add to what you have told me?'

They looked furtively at each other, and Miss Burton glanced towards Claydon; but that was all.

'You see, Hannah was older. And she never told us much about herself . . .'

He let them go, and they trooped away silently to collect their bags and coats. Claydon, who was smoking again, had begun stacking the account books in a pile.

'I still can't believe it . . . who would do such a thing? Not to mention the hole it's leaving me in . . .'

Gently snapped: 'Your accountant can sort that out.'

'But you don't understand. Those fellows cost money.'

'Weren't you paying Hannah Stoven?'

'They charge the earth. There's my wife too . . . she's an invalid. Do you know what a housekeeper costs these days? My hand is never out of my pocket.'

He jerked out a fresh cigarette, this time lighting it from the stub of the last. There was something disgusting about the way his eyes kept squinting towards the account books. Another lame duck . . . ? He had claimed to be fond of her, and yet, after the first shock was over . . . If his wife's invalidity were genuine, perhaps she had been poisoned by those cigarettes!

There was a thumping at the shop door, which the girls had locked as they left. Leyston went to investigate, and they heard a short exchange.

'It's Shavers with another man . . . Mason told them we were here.'

Gently glanced at Claydon.

'Better show them in.'

Claydon puffed meanly, but raised no objection.

Shavers had had time to spruce himself up and now looked more of a peacock – jazzy jacket, crewnecked sweater, mauve slacks and suede boots. His companion however wore fisherman's gear and gumboots with rolled tops. A heavy-shouldered, broad-faced man, he hung back as Shavers pushed into the office.

'Chiefie, listen – I've found you a witness.'

Gently met him with a bleak stare.

'What sort of a witness?'

'You'll see. This is Ted – Ted Moulton. He was up the river yesterday.'

'A customer of yours?'

'So what? I had to ask people who knew me, didn't I? I knew you weren't going to leave me alone till I could prove what I was telling you.'

'So you found a customer who fitted.'

'Ted, you tell him where you saw me. Then tell him what you saw when you were lifting your nets yesterday.'

He squeezed against the filing-cabinets to let the fisherman get by. Moulton brought into the office an odour of fish and beer to add to the fug of Claydon's cigarettes. Standing awkwardly, he blinked over Claydon's head at Gently. The bookseller drew back sharply, doubtless getting Moulton's smell at full strength.

'Well?'

'It's like Chick was telling you . . . I came up this way on yesterday's flood. And I saw Chick on his boat, doing something down below.'

'When was that?'

'Two, or just after. When the flood had started to make.'

'And you could see him – down below?'

'Well yes, that's right. I cocked my eye in as I was going by.'

'Was he there when you came back?'

'Well there you are . . . I didn't come down till the pubs turned out.'

'So you just saw him there at two, or a little after.'

'Yes . . . I can't say more than that.'

Gently stared across at Shavers. 'Scarcely worth the petrol, was it?'

'Chiefie, I was there – like I said I was!'

'And on top of the petrol, how many beers?'

'Never mind that, I was there – and someone bleeding saw me there. That's worth something, isn't it? And that isn't all by a long chalk.'

'So what else have you two been cooking up?'

'We haven't cooked up sodding nothing! I want you off my back, don't I? So I'm just giving the coppers a hand. You tell him, Ted.'

Moulton looked bemused and his moonish face was moist. A solid, shapeless figure, he loomed huge over the shrinking Claydon.

'I've got some nets up that way . . . in the drains, that's where they are.'

'Which drains?'

'What . . . ? In the bend, aren't they, just across from Bodney church. So I went up on the flood to draw them, and picked up nine or ten stone . . . then I came down to Friday's to get hold of Sam Yaxley.'

'Sam Yaxley?'

'He buys fish, doesn't he? He's got a cold-store up there. And after that I was in the Smacksman till they turned out, like I told you.'

'Why didn't you come straight home?'

'Why?' Moulton's eyes widened. 'You try coming down there against the flood, and see where that gets you, old matey.' He licked his lips. 'I'd as lief buy beer as petrol, and I don't care who knows it.'

'And that's all you have to tell me?'

'No it isn't.' He pressed up closer to the unhappy bookseller. 'Time I was up there after my nets I saw two boats on the other bank. One was a dinghy with an outboard motor and the other was a dinghy with a mast. They were pulled up together side by side, about quarter of a mile above Bodney church.'

Gently eyed the big fisherman, who nervously wiped his face with his sleeve. Shavers was dying to join in but, catching Gently's look, thought better of it.

'At what time was this?'

'Why, mid-afternoon . . . I can't rightly say when.'

'How long did you have the boats under observation?'

'I wasn't observing them at all, was I? I just cocked my eye in that direction, like you do when you're about. I was just leaving the topmost drain, so I'd be down out of sight in a couple of shakes. But there they were, side by side, one with a motor, one with a mast.'

'Did you recognise either of them?'

'Blast no. There's plenty like them about here. Chick's got one, only it couldn't have been him or I'd have seen him pass by me.'

'You see, Chiefie?' Shavers broke in. 'I'm covered. There's no bleeding way I could have been up there.'

Gently pinned him with a look. 'I've heard nothing that clears you, yet!'

'Chiefie, how could I have been there –'

'Keep quiet.'

'Yes, but listen, there's some more to come –'

'Just keep quiet.'

Shavers ducked his head, and Gently returned his attention to Moulton.

'Go on.'

Moulton mopped his face again; perhaps the beer was beginning to wear off. He swallowed a couple of times and then mumbled:

'I saw someone . . . a man.'

'Who?'

Moulton coughed, catching a puff of smoke from Claydon.

'I wouldn't know, would I? I mean, he wasn't nothing to me . . .'

'Where was he, and what was he doing?'

'He was just standing there, that's all.'

'Standing where?'

'Why, up at the road, where there's a path goes through the furze . . .'

'Describe him.'

Moulton began coughing again, but he couldn't avoid Claydon's smoke. Gasping, he got out:

'I couldn't make out his face, could I, but he was stumpy, dressed in something dark.'

'Stumpy, and dressed in something dark.'

'So it couldn't have been me!' Shavers broke in. 'You can't call me stumpy, and it's bleeding sure I don't dress like a funeral.'

'Shut up.'

'But for crying out loud –'

'Keep quiet, or I'll have you put out.'

Suddenly Claydon said, in a dry tone: 'It sounds very like a description of Group Captain Riddlesworth.'

'The Groupie – bloody yes!'

'Will you keep quiet?'

'But look, Chiefie, she knew a bloke with a yacht –'

'And this could be a pack of lies put together in the bar of the Eel's Foot!'

Now there was thunder in Gently's voice, and Shavers shut up as though he'd been struck. Moulton was breathing through his mouth, his eyes round, and Claydon squeezed small in his chair.

Thunder about . . . ! Even Leyston, hovering in the doorway, looked apprehensive.

Apologetically, Claydon murmured:

'I'm sorry. I shouldn't have said that.'

Gently ignored him. After a moment of silence, he said softly to Moulton:

'Do you know Group Captain Riddlesworth?'

'I . . . yes, I've seen him around.'

'And he resembles the man you saw yesterday?'

'Well . . . I don't know! . . . I aren't going to say that.'

'Why aren't you going to say it?'

Moulton's eyes were desperate. 'Look . . . I don't want to make trouble for no bugger! You've been at me to say what I saw, and that's what I saw, and that's all.'

'You saw a person of Group Captain Riddlesworth's description.'

'I aren't saying it was him, and that's flat.'

'But you want me to believe it was.'

'No! I haven't said nothing about the Group Captain.'

'Can you prove a single word of what you have been telling me?'

'Oh my lor'! Didn't I sell my fish yesterday?'

Fish he had evidently been in contact with lately: about that there could be no question. And he himself looked rather like a fish, gaping and squirming at the end of a line.

Gently shrugged wearily.

'Give your address to the Inspector, and clear out.'

'It's the God's honest truth I've told you –'

'Get out before I change my mind!'

Moulton got out, but his odour still lingered in that cupboard of an office. Shavers continued to hover by the cabinets, his eyes fixed cautiously on Gently.

'Listen, Chiefie –'

'Come here, you.'

Reluctantly, Shavers advanced a couple of steps. Neither paid any attention to the bookseller, who sat crouched between them, his head well down.

'Now bear this in mind! The next witness you bring me had better be cold sober, and no customer of yours. Just this once I'm going to pretend that he wasn't bribed and wasn't primed. But next time I shall throw the book at you – and leave Myrtle to pick up the pieces.'

'So help me, Chiefie, I didn't prime him . . . I might have bought him a few beers.'

'And helped his memory!'

'Honest to God, I only told him he must have seen me on the yacht.'

'But he didn't, did he?'

'Well, he wasn't sure . . . but all the rest is straight up. When he told me about the boats I rushed him straight round here, I knew you'd want to hear about that.'

'And about the Group Captain?'

'He just told me a man. I didn't ask for a sodding description.'

Gently gave him an incredulous look.

'All right – that's all for now!'

Shavers hastened after his friend, and Leyston let them out into the night. Claydon sat straighter in his chair and, with shaky fingers, lit one more cigarette.

'Could it be true – about the Group Captain?'

'You had better forget what you've just heard.'

'I'm no gossip, but all the same . . .' He took a lungful of smoke straight down. 'Is that fellow a suspect?'

'I said, forget it.'

Leyston had come back to stand in the doorway; he sniffed the atmosphere once or twice. Claydon was squinting at the account books again.

5

Had Gently really taken over that case, lock and stock, shouldering poor Leyston to one side? If he had not, then now was surely the time to bow out gracefully and get back to his paint-brushes. He had opened the affair up; that afternoon, virtually all Leyston had got was a corpse. Now, Gently had laid out the groundwork, stirring up leads that an application of routine would probably make productive. It was as much as the Chief Constable had asked, and more – and no doubt that Leyston was itching to get rid of him!

Only . . . was it quite so simple?

Gently brooded over the matter as they headed away from the bookshop. For example, in Capel he had a pick-lock to the local society who was probably unavailable to Leyston. Then there was Shavers, an element that Leyston might find himself ill-equipped to handle; while on the horizon, shaping plainer and plainer, was a man who might baffle him altogether. The real battle was about to begin: was it fair to leave the local man to cope on his own?

At the door of the police station, he hesitated.

'Is there a pub that serves decent food?'

'There's the Smacksman . . . I was calling there anyway.'

'Like that, we can kill two birds with one stone.'

The Smacksman was a pub on the town's narrow prom-enade, close to the shingle and the lifeboat station. There, sitting with bread and cheese and a pint, he watched Leyston tackle the locals: first the landlord, then a group of darts-players, among whom was a hard-framed man with pitted features.

'That fellow is Yaxley, the wholesaler . . . he confirms what Moulton told us. So does Neal, the landlord, who knows Moulton well.'

'Sit down and help yourself to a snack.'

'I was thinking I ought to get back to the station.'

'This will give you time to think. That's part of the job, too.'

Leyston ate and drank hungrily, but if he was thinking his thoughts were gloomy, and several times Gently caught the local inspector eyeing him uncertainly. Leyston was no fool. He could probably see what was lying ahead as clearly as Gently, and obviously he wasn't liking what he saw. At the same time, it was Leyston's case . . .

Finally, Gently glanced at his watch.

'I shall have to get back. My wife is expecting a call from me, later.'

Leyston received the announcement in silence, his face if possible growing longer.

'You will need to cross-check on Shavers and turn up anyone who was using that back road yesterday afternoon. And at the same time keep probing around until you identify the boy friend.'

Leyston drank up.

'Does that mean I won't be seeing you again . . . sir?'

'It's your case,' Gently shrugged.

Leyston gazed into his mug.

'I was hoping that perhaps . . .'

'Perhaps . . . ?'

'Well sir, the Group Captain . . . I shall need to talk to him.'

And that was it. Leyston ventured a glance, then went on staring at the mug.

'You'd like to have me sit in?'

'It's this way, sir . . . I'm local here, but you aren't. I could put my foot in it, but with you it doesn't matter one way or the other.'

'You're forgetting I'm local too, now.'

'You know what I mean, sir – you're the Yard.'

'I doubt if that will cut much ice with Riddlesworth.'

'All the same, sir . . . if you can spare the time . . .'

What Leyston was never going to admit was that he, Gently, would be starting on something like equal terms, while Leyston, the local man, stood every chance of being brushed aside. To Leyston, the Group Captain must look formidable, the retired hero who was also a big noise, and perhaps even a sidekick of the Chief Constable's. What it called for was talent from town!

'Riddlesworth did say he wanted to help us.'

'That's what he'd say in any case, sir.'

'So we'll take him at his word.'

'As I see it, sir, he's *got* to know something.'

Gently nodded: at every turn, there had been pointers towards Riddlesworth, from Capel, the bookseller and the girls down to the suspect evidence of Moulton. The Group Captain had questions to answer . . . though whether he would answer them was a different matter.

'Very well. We'll see him together.'

In his sad-faced way, Leyston looked relieved.

'If you're free in the morning . . .'

Gently shook his head. 'The evening is still young – we'll see him tonight.'

Down at the Maltings the mist was now so thick that Gently had to grind along in second, while the floodlit face of the inn was barely visible as they crept by. Just there, the road faded into the yard where the lorries pulled in to load and unload, and into this they must have strayed, since suddenly Gently was standing on his brakes to avoid hitting a wall.

'It's the wall of his garden . . . safe to park here, sir.'

Outside the mist was raw and smelled of decay. For a moment Gently was completely disoriented, but then he found the wall again and could feel his way along it. They came to open wrought-iron gates, gravel that crunched, and at last steps leading to a door. Leyston rang, and a light fizzed above them. It was Riddlesworth himself who answered the ring.

'Hullo . . . isn't it a bit late for you fellows?'

'If we could just have a word, sir.'

Riddlesworth stared at them flatly for a second, then stood back to let them in.

They entered a warm, well-furnished hall with a carpet laid over coloured tiles, from which a staircase with wrought-iron rails led to a lounge-landing. Riddlesworth however led them along smartly to a door at the end of the hall. He switched on lights, and they found themselves in a room lined with books.

'My private sanctum.'

He closed the door and pointed to two chairs. Besides the books, framed photographs and paintings of aircraft occupied the walls. A big desk was covered with papers and beside it stood two filing-cabinets. On a stand, on a small table, stood a silver model of a four-engined bomber.

Riddlesworth strutted across to the latter and spun the propellers.

'Do you recognise the mark?'

'A Halifax,' Gently shrugged.

'The finest heavy bomber of them all.'

And in fact, when you looked round the room, every picture and photograph was of the same aircraft, each in its wartime livery of camouflage and black. Some were flying, some parked on dispersals, some had covers drooping from their engines. On the ground they looked particularly menacing, with their noses and engines cocked high.

'You remember the Halys?'

'I remember them.'

Riddlesworth took the model from its stand. He held it up as though it were in flight, his almost lidless eyes caressing it.

'I'd back a Halibasher against the world . . . it's because of a Haly that I'm alive today. You could shoot them to bits and they'd still hang together . . . yet some people have forgotten they ever existed.'

'All the publicity went to the Lancaster . . .'

'The Lanc was a cow, you can take it from me. It hadn't the guts – look at this airframe, the strength of the lines, the wings, the fins. This was an aircraft to do a job, and take its medicine if it had to. Do you know what I'm up to? I'm writing a book to give the Haly its proper place in history.'

'To settle a bet . . . weren't there one or two Halifaxes equipped with Hercules engines?'

'You're absolutely right. In fact, I had the offer of one, but turned it down because the handling was different. And that's odd, when you come to think of it, since I was brought up on Peggies and Hercs. Remember Peggies? They had that little whistle, like a bird twittering to itself in flight . . .'

He was gazing fondly at the model, when in a flash it happened: Gently found himself staring at a different man. It was almost eerie; over the tight, frozen features floated the mask of a handsome youngster, full-mouthed, frank-eyed, brown hair falling over a determined brow. Like a ghost it hovered about the sub-structure, the cruel caricature left behind by the surgeons: the ghost of a young man who had retreated behind the eyes, but who now, in a moment of enthusiasm, had rematerialised.

Involuntarily, Gently blurted out:

'In those days . . . did you drive an M.G.?'

'What? It was an S.S. actually, a lovely little car that went like a bomb. Ever drive one?'

Gently shook his head.

'I've stayed with the marque. Now I drive a Jag.'

Had Leyston noticed? Probably not; the Shinglebourne inspector sat twiddling his hands. This was Gently's picnic, his attitude said: he, Leyston, was accepting his role of passenger.

But Hannah – wouldn't she have noticed it, with that sympathy that could extend even to a Shavers . . . and wouldn't that ghost have rushed to materialise in the kind light of her eyes?

'Was yours a wartime marriage?'

'Sue was the daughter of my first C.O. on squadron. Sue Gresham. We were married with a full turnout and an armed guard of erks. But mostly it was services of another kind in those days, with a bugler and a volley over the grave . . .'

'For her, it must have been a harrowing time.'

Without a moment's hesitation Riddlesworth pointed to his face.

'You mean this?'

'Among other things.'

'Yes . . . well, Sue was an officer's daughter.'

He blew on the model, setting the props spinning.

'Actually, I did offer Sue an out. But she was a brick, she stood by me, and it's turned out pretty well. We've got three children, two boys and a girl. Girl's married to an underwriter in the city. Eldest son is training fighter-pilots. Youngest is studying to be a composer.'

'Music means a lot to you.'

'If Mark has talent, it certainly doesn't come from me. Rattling off *In the Mood* on the mess piano was the limit of my achievement.'

'But music is important.'

'I do my best to go on building up the Festival.'

'Hannah Stoven was a violinist.'

Riddlesworth's eyes flickered. 'Yes. What a bloody waste of talent.'

'She did have talent, then?'

'She was wasting it, anyway . . .'

'Did you ever hear her play?'

'Yes, once.'

'Where was that?'

His eyes were quite steady. 'Up at her place.'

'I hadn't heard she invited people there.'

'Well . . . once she invited me. We used to talk music. There was a Brahms score which I never knew existed. She had it. One of the dances. She took me back and played it to me. Marvellous. She was as good as her father in my humble opinion.'

'Did you try to encourage her?'

'What do you think? And Capel tried to inveigle her into his lot. No use. She was shy as a gazelle when it came to a public performance.'

'Yet . . . she played for you.'

'Once.'

'It still puts you in a special category.'

Riddlesworth ran his fingers along the row of propellers.

'I say! I haven't yet offered you fellows a drink.'

A decanter, siphon and glasses stood on a tray on a sidetable, and Riddlesworth, without enquiring about individual tastes, mixed three whisky-and-sodas.

'Here's mud.'

He threw back his drink and returned the glass to the tray. Then he picked up the model again and came to take a chair facing Gently's.

'You know, I've had a word with Sir Tom about you.'

Gently was scarcely surprised. 'You know him?'

'Pretty well. He's a Festival buff and he lives at Earl's Newton, a few miles off. Says you're pretty top brass at the Yard and I should watch my step. Would you say that was true?'

Gently sipped his drink.

'So what exactly do you want with me?'

There was no young man showing in the face now: just the mask the surgeons had created, tight, frozen, with the mouth a gash.

Gently said mildly: 'We're questioning everyone who we think may be able to help us.'

'I'm all for that, of course. But precisely how does it apply to me?'

'It would be useful to know when you last saw Hannah.'

'I doubt if it would, but I'm game. It was two days ago, in town. I met her on her way to Claydon's. Then I saw her again a little later, when I was enquiring after a book.'

'You had conversation with her?'

'Just chit-chat.'

'About what?'

'Oh, this and that. Mostly about the book I'm hunting for, which contains an account of the early daylight raids.'

'The book is waiting for you.'

'Really?'

'Yesterday, Hannah was apparently expecting to meet you.

The book had come in, and Hannah told Claydon that if she saw you, she would let you know.'

Riddlesworth sawed the model back and forth.

'Well, she didn't see me, and that's flat.'

'But why would she expect she might?'

'Couldn't say. Unless she thought I would be down at the yacht club.'

'But you no longer keep a yacht.'

'I still look in there. Old habits die hard.'

'So that often you met her there?'

'Sometimes. But yesterday wasn't one of them.'

'She never told you about the book.'

He shook his head abruptly.

'Yesterday afternoon, you didn't see her?'

'No.'

'It might help to have your movements from, say, after lunch yesterday.'

The thin line of Riddlesworth's mouth curled crookedly, and he performed a number of the manoeuvres with the model. He wasn't going to be rushed; behind his mask he was clearly testing a decision. Yet, for all his seeming straightforwardness, one had to set a question mark beside Riddlesworth. If he had to lie, it would probably be with the same firm assurance with which he told the truth.

'I couldn't prove them, you know.'

'That may not matter.'

'As a suspect, I'd be a sitting duck.'

'We are simply seeking your help.'

'Nice of you to say so, but I've sat on a few court-martials in my time. I can see your point of view. I knew the girl over a period and even visited her at her home. She was attractive, sympathetic, and might even have been persuaded to overlook this.' He gestured to his face. 'And then – one thing leading to another – she might easily have become a problem. You may think I am a man with something to lose, not to mention a penny in the bank. That's a reasonable assessment, isn't it? I wouldn't blame you for making it.'

Gently said evenly: 'We look at all the possibilities.'

'You would be a fool if you didn't. And – though you haven't met Sue – she would certainly have entered your calculations. I told you that she stood by me, but how long does one stand by a man like myself? Ten years? Twenty? In the end, wouldn't loyalty wear a little thin? So I would be easy meat for a young lady like Hannah, who might well have had ambitions to be the second Mrs Riddlesworth. Then I would have been at a crossroads, wouldn't I? And I'm a man who has seen a bit of violence.'

'You might also have been disturbed if she had threatened to break it off.'

Riddlesworth gave the model a jerk.

'I didn't think of that.'

'And perhaps more disturbed if she were throwing you over for another.'

He started toying with the model again, making it sweep up and down in dives and climbs. No, you couldn't rush him! He was used to taking time to look all round a proposition. That had been his training: when the chips were down to stay cool, take the right decision . . .

'Do you remember the Stirling?'

Gently said nothing.

'The Stirling was a brute of a kite . . . electrical undercart. They lost more Stirlings on circuits and bumps than they did on ops. Some structural weakness too. I saw one come down through cloud cover in a steep dive, pull out too flat and break its back, snapping it off clean at the taper . . . curtains all round, of course, and a bloody great hole in a field. Problem was we didn't know if it was carrying a bomb-load. Three-oh-three going off in all directions.'

'What did you do?'

'Poured in foam regardless. Fire crew deserved medals, but didn't get them.'

'Where were you?'

'Directing the sods. It happened on a day when I was duty officer.'

Gently sipped his drink, and Leyston, from the sidelines, contributed a dry little cough. Riddlesworth continued to make swoops with the model, apparently to illustrate the incident he had just related.

'War is one thing, strangling girls another.'

'Who told you that Hannah was strangled?'

'Saw it. I was down on the quay when the fellow towed her in. He's clear, is he?'

Gently watched him.

'Believe it or not, but I bloody wept. I came back here and had a couple of drinks and sat blubbing in that chair. I couldn't tell Sue.'

'Had your wife met her?'

'Hannah and her father too. They were at the Festival. Girl was happy then, when she was going about with her father.'

'Wasn't she happy at other times?'

'She put a good face on it, but there was something missing underneath. She had never come to terms with being an exile, that's my opinion of Hannah.'

'Yet she had been here since she was twelve . . .'

'She had never settled. She and her father spoke Czech all the time. Her English was good, but the accent terrible. She bought everything in Czech she could lay her hands on.'

'Frankly, was she your mistress?'

Riddlesworth blew on the propellers. 'You may ask me questions that I may not answer. And you can make what you like of that.'

'Hannah had a lover.'

'Can you prove it?'

'In May, she sought a pregnancy test.'

'In May . . . ?'

'Does that mean something to you?'

He shook his head and went on blowing.

'She had been with a man just before her death.'

'Is that to say you think he did it?'

'Did you know that she had an acquaintance at Harford, a man whose yacht she used to visit?'

Now his eyes did latch on Gently's!

'If she had a lover, she never told me. Who was he?'

'Had you no suspicion? You seem to have been in her company as much as most people.'

'Well, I hadn't, it never occurred to me. And I think you may be having me on.'

'We know the rendezvous where they met.'

'Then you must have talked to someone.'

'Hannah and he had been meeting all through the summer.'

'I don't think you know who he is at all.'

'I could give you a name.'

The model was staying quite still, and Riddlesworth had dropped his eyes to it. One more of those careful pauses, while his mind sifted through all the possibilities! It was infuriating that the frozen face could remain so empty of every emotion.

'So give me his name.'

'Perhaps I may. The meetings continued up to yesterday.'

'When – he killed her?'

'What we know is that she died then or very shortly afterwards.'

'I still don't know if you're having me on. Don't forget I was warned you were a tricky customer.'

'You were going to give me your movements for yesterday afternoon.'

'To quote yourself, perhaps I may.'

Riddlesworth rested the model on his knee while he pierced and lit a cheroot. He did it with the decisive movements that were characteristic of the man. With Claydon, a fresh cigarette was a symptom of nervousness and his tremulous hands betrayed it: not so with Riddlesworth. His hands were firm and he puffed at the cheroot with calm indifference. If he had ever been captured, number, rank and name would have been the sum of information they would have got from him. At sixty he carried a little more weight, but his steely will remained intact.

'All right then – it's no mystery. I told you that I am working on a book. That's it on the desk. From lunch till tea I was sitting there typing and checking references. Ever write a book?'

'Just reports.'

'Ah yes. Then you'll know it's the biggest sweat going. Especially this sort, when they'll be at my throat if I make the smallest error of fact. Checking references takes most of the time, even though I know my facts by heart.'

'After lunch you came here.'

'Right.'

'Who was with you at lunch?'

'Sue and Mark – that's my youngest. He pops in here from the school.'

'You left them to come here?'

'Left Sue clearing dishes. Mark had a lecture period, he'd gone, and Sue left half an hour later.'

'To go where?'

'To the church, which is at the other end of the village. Tomorrow is the harvest festival service and Sue always gives a hand with the decorations.'

'When did she leave?'

'Say fourteen hundred.'

'Did she look in on you before she left?'

'Right.'

'When did she return?'

'Better ask her. About seventeen hundred.'

'And your son?'

'Same time.'

'No doubt you employ a domestic help.'

'A couple, Mrs Lane from Ivy Cottage and Molly Turner from Tinker's Green. They stay late when we're entertaining but otherwise leave at thirteen hundred. Then there's the gardener, Jack Willis, who lives in The Cot, Marsh Road. He comes three days a week, but yesterday wasn't one of them.'

'So that between two and five p.m. yesterday nobody can vouch for your presence here.'

'Not a soul. I did tell you that I couldn't prove my movements.'

He took several smooth puffs and stared firmly at Gently: straight questions, straight answers, without a hint of evasion or impatience. So why did one feel an air of challenge about him, a sensation that he was getting his shots in first, as though he might be standing guard over something that Gently wasn't even going to be allowed to glimpse?

One question only he had refused to answer: whether Hannah Stoven had been his mistress.

'Would you know the time of low slack water yesterday?'

'Naturally.' The corner of his slit mouth twisted. 'When you live here you get the tide in your veins, especially if you happen to be a yachtsman.'

'When was it?'

'From fourteen to fifteen hundred.'

'At that time, you could sail a small boat downstream?'

'Why not? The wind was nor'-west, two to three. Give you a broad reach down to Bodney church and a comfortable haul coming back.'

'Why to Bodney church?'

'You would meet the flood there, and without an engine you'd be stuck. The flood runs at three to four knots. You'd be standing still or going backwards.'

'But you could get to Bodney church?'

'Check.'

'In a dinghy such as that pulled up on your foreshore?'

'No problem.'

'It being apparently the only sailing dinghy that just now is based at Thwaite.'

'As far as I know.'

Riddlesworth blew smoke at the model to set the four propellers spinning afresh. If Gently was getting through to him, then that was the only indication.

'The dinghy was seen near the church.'

'My dinghy?'

'You tell me there is no other based up here.'

'It could have come up from the town.'

Gently shook his head. 'It would need to have beaten up

against the ebb to have been where it was when sighted.'

'Who saw it there?'

'We have a witness. And the dinghy wasn't all he saw.'

'You make it sound intriguing.'

'What I want to know is, what your dinghy was doing there at that time.'

'So do I – if it was my dinghy. Mark was at classes and Sue at the church. It would mean that some charlie sneaked through the grounds here and went for an illicit sail.'

'It would mean that?'

'No other explanation. I never shifted from that desk.'

'I wish you could prove that.'

'I wish so too. But I've already explained that I can't.'

He didn't even bother to sound indignant, much less fly into loud assertions. It was merely a point to be taken and disposed of, then followed by a casual puff or two.

A stonewaller . . .

But still you had the feeling that, behind the bat, lay a vulnerable wicket.

'Your wife has her own car?'

'A small Peugeot. A likeable little beast.'

'And your son?'

'Mark sticks to his pushbike. He goes camping with it, too.'

'Yesterday afternoon, your own car would have been available.'

'Right. But what is all this about cars?'

'Would you care to describe it?'

For once Riddlesworth checked, as though Gently had got on to unexpected ground.

'You can see it if you like. It's an XJS-HE. I took delivery of the brute two months ago. They've fixed it up with some new gubbins to improve consumption and I can get twenty-two with a mean foot.'

'Colour?'

'White.'

He still wasn't happy.

'Did you drive it at all yesterday?'

'Yes – I did. Just into the town to pick up some booze, and this and that.'

'In the morning?'

'When else?'

'So that in the afternoon it never left your garage.'

'That is precisely the case.'

'Would you object to telling me what clothes you were wearing yesterday?'

Riddlesworth considered the model again, apparently manoeuvring it through a spin. The cheroot was stuck in his mouth and little runlets of smoke were escaping from his nostrils.

'You're asking some damned rum questions, but I'll go along. I was wearing a blazer and slacks.'

'What colour slacks?'

'Navy.'

'Shirt?'

'A tan shirt, blast it.'

'A man was observed watching the sailing dinghy and Mrs Stoven's dinghy, which was moored beside it. He is described as being below average height and dressed in dark clothing.'

Riddlesworth puffed and played, eyes, face wholly blank. If anything it was Leyston who was feeling the pressure, and who stirred furtively, and examined his hands. From their entry, the house itself had been silent, though one could hear distant vehicles moaning by through the mist.

At last Riddlesworth removed his cheroot and looked about for an ashtray to flick it in.

'Nice try.'

'Is that your only comment?'

On second thoughts he stubbed the cheroot.

'I don't know who your man was, but it wasn't me. I was sitting here suffering all afternoon. My car was in the garage, Sue's was at the church and Mark's pushbike was down at the school. And, to the best of my knowledge, the dinghy was sitting on its chocks on the foreshore.'

'One or another of those statements is false.'

'Show me different and I stand corrected.'

'I would like to speak to your wife and your son.'

Riddlesworth took sight along the model.

'You can talk to Sue, but Mark's away – he went off with his tent this morning.'

'Went off where?'

'Sorry, but I don't have that information.'

Neither did Mrs Riddlesworth, a sharp-featured blonde who stood almost a head taller than her husband. Dressed in a gown with a choke throat, she appeared promptly at his bidding. She had caught his manner, and answered questions with the same bold curtness, her accent suggesting a finishing school and a certainty of being listened to.

'Harry was working in here when I left and was still working when I returned . . . I arrived at the church at two-ten and was back again before five. Harry's car was in the garage on each occasion, when I fetched mine and when I returned it. Mark went to his class at one-forty-five and was in the house when I got back.'

'Did you speak to him this morning?'

'Certainly.'

'Didn't he tell you where he was going?'

'No.'

'Was that usual?'

'Quite usual. I made certain that he took sufficient food.'

'But surely you have some idea of where he was heading?'

'Pretty well where his fancy took him, I imagine. We have never been over-protective with our brats. As a result, they are very self-dependent.'

'At other times, where has he gone?'

'Is it so important that you talk to him?'

'I would like to have his account of yesterday.'

'Well, for the life of me I can't think why.'

Hands in the blazer pockets, Riddlesworth stood by, never once prompting or offering support. Gently was welcome, he seemed to be saying, whatever he could get out of Sue he'd deserve . . .

'When your son does return, I wish to see him.'

'I'll give you a ring,' Riddlesworth said. 'Will that be everything?'

'Everything for now. But I may have to talk to you again.'

'Any time I can be of real help you can depend on me, and I mean that.'

He saw them to the door and switched on a drive-lamp that helped them fumble their way to the gate. The mist seemed to have got thicker, if that were possible, and they had to cast about to locate the car.

6

Driving out of that pestilential mist was like abruptly emerging from a bank of cloud; at one moment they were creeping through a luminous nowhere, at the next road, trees and cottages sprang to life in their headlights. The moon had risen, and once clear of the village they could see the white coverlet of the mist below them, blanking out the river and the wide spread of the marshes as far as a rim of distant high ground. Last night it must have been the same, and under just such a coverlet had Hannah's dinghy drifted: a plaything of the tides that moved this way and that at the moon's discretion. Had Riddlesworth known it was there when, last night, he had locked his door? Or Shavers, across at his pub in Harford, when, the last glass rinsed, he had retired upstairs with Myrtle? Somewhere, someone had been trying to behave normally, while knowing the discovery the next day must bring: going through routine, and perhaps overplaying in an effort not to appear different. Wouldn't anyone have noticed? Probably not. They would have put it down to drink or to a cold just starting . . . until next day they heard the news, when still they would be reluctant to make the connection.

It had happened before, even with multiple killers, and when facts were staring people in the face . . .

'You must find that kid and get his story.'

Because that was the one thing the memsahib had dropped: that when she had returned from the church yesterday, she had found her son already in the house. How long had he been there, and how much did he know? His absence camping might be quite innocent: but it was one way of concealing an inconvenient witness, and at least of buying time.

'I'll enquire at the music school first thing.'

Leyston had spotted the slip too. Though he had sat glum-faced through the interview, he had been following each move with jealous attention.

'On Friday they might finish early, sir, and perhaps only have a single period.'

'Check the camp sites in the district. On a bicycle, he couldn't have got far.'

'If he knew his father was out, and we get to him first . . .'

Gently clamped hard on the stem of his pipe. Not for a long time had a man disturbed him as much as Group Captain Riddlesworth! He had come away from the house feeling completely unsettled, with his mind in a turmoil. Against a set of facts, pointing all one way, had been set an assurance that seemed almost superhuman. Could any man lie as well as that? Hadn't Riddlesworth, indeed, been overplaying? Gently couldn't make up his mind, and the vacillation was gnawing at him. He growled:

'Check the wife's movements too. Nothing would surprise me about a pair like that.'

'Do you think she had a hand in it?'

'The Lord knows. But don't leave anything to chance.'

'If she had found him together with the girl . . .'

Yes, there were all sorts of permutations – including the innocence of all parties: except that Riddlesworth had almost certainly been Hannah's lover.

'From somewhere, you'll have to dig up witnesses – cast-iron testimony about Riddlesworth's movements. If he was seen in his car or dinghy, if his car was noticed parked at the rendez-vous. And that goes for his wife too: if she was seen anywhere in the vicinity.'

'What about Shavers?'

Gently grunted impatiently – beside Riddlesworth, Shavers was wellnigh transparent.

'Don't waste too much manpower on him. Leave the local constable to check him out.'

But even as he said it he felt a surge of resentment that Riddlesworth should thus be engrossing the scene, and perhaps seducing his attention from a suspect worthy of more consideration. Confound the man! Back there, hadn't he been tacitly issuing a challenge – summing up the case against himself, and more or less defying Gently to trap him?

He had baulked at only the one question, whether or not he had been Hannah's lover: but couldn't that have been pure mischief too, calculated to keep Gently simmering in uncertainty?

On the other hand the date of the pregnancy test had made him hesitate, just for an instant . . .

'Shall I see you tomorrow, sir?'

They had arrived at the police station, and Leyston was waiting with his hand on the door. Somewhere down the line, that evening, he had resigned himself to the situation for good.

'Don't forget that I'm still unofficial.'

But that was ducking the issue, and he knew it.

Hesitating, Leyston said: 'I am grateful, sir . . .'

Then after a moment, he closed the door.

Gently was still churning over his resentment when he parked the Princess in the coach-house at Heatherings, but then the soothing atmosphere of the mellow house, and all it meant, began to steal over him. It was as though he were turned about face, with all that day's fret pushed to a distance – he was home; and in a way that had never been the case in the villa in North London. There one had merely enjoyed a respite, some hours off from the daily grind, liable at any moment to be called out or to have colleagues hunting one down. Well, he had been called out here too, but that had been voluntary and different. It wasn't his case: he could drop it right there, to read about it some time in a local paper . . .

He let himself in, and switched on lights to admire his handiwork in the hall. Then the kitchen door opened to spill forth the sound of some TV quiz programme.

'Someone rang and left a message, Mr George.'

His stare at Mrs Jarvis was less than friendly.

'Who?'

'Gave the name of Claydon, and said he'd be calling round later on.'

Without a word, Gently went through to the lounge to pour himself a drink. So even here you couldn't rely on privacy, on slamming the office door when you came in!

'Something to eat, Mr George?'

Mrs Jarvis had followed him, perhaps concerned by her chilly reception.

'Just coffee and a wedge of parkin.'

In half an hour, he was due to make his call to Gabrielle.

He went through to the kitchen for his coffee and tried to interest himself in the TV programme, at the same time wondering, for the umpteenth time, why the BBC classified its patrons as morons. And wouldn't it have to be Claydon! That unattractive moppet whose only enthusiasm was for his account books, a shrivelled soul: why must he pester Gently, and at this end of the evening?

As though it had been arranged, the doorbell rang just as Gently was picking up the phone. For an exasperated moment he remained undecided, then strode to the door and flung it open. Claydon stood blinking at him, his foxy face apprehensive.

'What is it you want?'

'I've got to talk to you . . . I'm sorry it's so late.'

'Won't it do tomorrow?'

'No it won't. I promise not to take up very much of your time.'

'If it's about the investigation you should talk to Leyston. My capacity is advisory.'

'It's because of that I've come to you. There is something I would like you to understand.'

In the end, Gently took him into the lounge and sat him down. Certainly the fellow was looking upset; his first act was to jerk off his glasses and give them a polish.

'Look – I can't give you very long.'

'I'm sorry. My glasses were misted . . .'

'Just why have you come here?'

'Because ... but I don't want you to think that I'm afraid.'

'Afraid of what?'

Claydon blinked rapidly. 'That man Shavers came back to the shop. He was alone this time, but his manner was threatening, and he more or less accused me.'

'He did, did he?'

'Yes. He swore that if I'd done it, he'd have me. He said that his own head was on the block, and that he would stop at nothing to clear himself. Well, I'm not a coward, but I don't mind admitting that a character like that could beat me up. He's a criminal of some sort, of that I'm certain, and I gathered he'd been through your hands before . . .'

Poor little man. On the edge of a chair, he sat quivering and trying to talk bold, while behind the glasses his eyes jittered and a bony hand gripped each knee.

'Smoke if you want to.'

'Thanks.'

He wasted no time in lighting up. Gently found him an ashtray, then himself lit a pipe.

'Are you asking for protection?'

'No . . . that is, perhaps you could have a word with him. I mean, if he comes there when the shop is open, making accusations and behaving violently . . .'

'Did he act violently?'

'He was threatening. He talked of smashing me and breaking my neck. He didn't actually get hold of me, but he stood over me making threatening gestures.'

'What gave him the idea that you might be the man?'

'Because I was Hannah's employer, I suppose! He'd got to know that my wife is an invalid, and in his stupid brain that meant I'd be keeping a mistress. Keep a mistress – I can scarcely keep myself. By the end of the month I could be insolvent. And he couldn't have known Hannah very well to make an absurd suggestion like that . . .'

'He claims to have been fond of her, too.'

'That's sickening, and I don't believe it. What would

Hannah have to do with a vulgar criminal, which I'm pretty certain is what he is. No, if anyone's guilty, it's Shavers, he fits the part like a glove. Though I'm making no accusations, mind . . . I daresay you've got this little matter in hand.'

It was almost comedy. Finding Gently with Claydon, Shavers had jumped to the conclusion that Claydon was the culprit, while Claydon, listening to their exchanges, had jumped to the conclusion it was Shavers.

And now Gently had to keep the peace between these two alarmed people . . .

'Why didn't you go to Leyston?'

'Obviously you were the man in charge. I won't say I doubt Inspector Leyston's ability, but in the past I have never found him very sympathetic.'

'If you want protection he's the man to give it.'

'Well, I didn't want to go to him for that. I'm not scared personally, please understand. It's the effect on the business I'm bothered about.'

'Of course.'

'I'm in enough trouble, and this sort of thing is scarcely good for trade. Will it get into the papers?'

'I'm afraid so.'

Claydon sucked nervously, his face twitching.

'It's this recession . . . I've had a terrible summer, even the Festival let me down. Usually it sees me through to the Christmas trade, but this year – I don't know!'

'Is that all you have to tell me?'

'No – not exactly.'

He crushed the cigarette and started on another. Whatever his problems with VAT, he was taking the tobacco tax in his stride.

'Before I set out, the telephone rang.'

He edged forward on the chair.

'It was the Group Captain. I gathered you'd been out there. He wanted to ask me a lot of questions. And I can't help it, I'm feeling guilty, because I'm certain it's what I said that put you on to him.'

He glanced pathetically at Gently, who sat puffing at his largest pipe.

'Wasn't it that?'

'Not entirely. We do make up our own minds.'

'But what I said must have settled it. If it was him who was seen there, then you couldn't not ask him what he was doing. Stupidly, I came out with his name . . . I could have kicked myself. He's a good customer.'

'Why did you come out with it?'

'I don't know . . . because we'd been talking about him and Hannah. It was out of my mouth before I realised. And the description could have been of anyone.'

'The description fitted him.'

'But it was vague.'

'Yet at once you thought of Riddlesworth.'

Claydon was becoming agitated. He jerked his cigarette, dropping ash on the lounge's new carpet.

'I can't explain it. It just came out because you'd been asking questions about him.'

'It wasn't because, for example, you knew more about Riddlesworth than you'd chosen to admit – about a good customer?'

'But what more could I know?'

'Perhaps you'd seen them together on more than the one occasion, and when their demeanour was rather different. Or perhaps Hannah talked, back there in the office.'

'That's ridiculous.'

'It's a cosy little office. In there you're sitting knee to knee. Just the place for a confidential chat . . . especially when the girls were occupied with customers.'

'That's a stupid insinuation!'

'Wouldn't you have talked to her?'

'But it didn't need to be . . . what you're suggesting.'

'What am I suggesting?'

'What . . . ? The same thing that Shavers was hinting at, earlier!' He seemed thoroughly upset, his lips quivering so that he had to remove the cigarette. 'I had to take such talk from

Shavers, but I hardly expected to hear it from you.'

'Calm yourself, Mr Claydon.'

'Yes, I'm sorry. But it really is too much.'

'I only wished to know if she confided in you about Riddlesworth.'

'She didn't mention him at all.'

'In fact, all you know about him you've told me.'

'I've told you everything I remember.'

He pulled the glasses off again, and, after wiping them, dabbed his eyes. Without them his face looked oddly incomplete, rather like a plant that had been growing behind a stone. He jammed them back on with a little jerky movement, then rescued his cigarette.

'What you don't understand is that I feel shocked about it. Hannah meant a good deal to me. Perhaps that's why it hurts when people go about suggesting . . .'

'There was never anything of that sort between you.'

'Never. I treated Hannah with every respect.'

'Just . . . friendliness.'

'You believe me, don't you?'

'What were the questions that Riddlesworth was asking?'

'Oh – those.'

He seemed put out afresh and, as usual, took refuge in hearty puffs. His every reaction was slightly eccentric, as though he were governed by some chronic inhibition.

'Well, he asked me very much the same as you did. Whether I knew the name of Hannah's lover. Whether I had suggested any names to you, and if you were sure of the exact spot where it happened.'

'He asked that specifically?'

'He did.'

'What did you tell him?'

Claydon puffed rapidly. 'Perhaps I shouldn't have answered that, but I was feeling guilty about having put you on to him. I repeated what the fisherman told you about seeing the two boats and the man.'

'Did you tell him the fisherman's name?'

'I didn't remember it. But I did say that his evidence was suspect. So I had to mention Shavers too, and he wanted to know all about him. Then . . . I don't know! He began to question me and make insinuations, just like Shavers – asking me to account for my movements, and trying to catch me with trick questions. I suppose it was a quid pro quo, because he must have guessed that it was me who mentioned him to you, but by the time he had finished I was quite limp. I'd sooner answer your questions than his.'

'Were you able to convince him?'

'Well . . . yes! My movements yesterday are quite account-able. I was at the business as usual, and out buying in the afternoon.'

'Out buying . . . ?'

'At Russell's, of Southgate. He had some local books to sell. They included a Suckling's *Suffolk*.' Claydon flickered him a look. 'I don't suppose you'd be interested?'

'When were you there?'

'When?' The bookseller's eyes widened. 'Look . . . you can ring Russell, and ask him. Here's his appointment, for four p.m.'

He pulled out a wallet which was bulging, not with notes, but with letters, one of which he selected and held out to Gently. It was a letter from an antique dealer, and confirmed the appointment.

'Look, if I'm under suspicion too, perhaps I shouldn't be talking so openly.'

'All Hannah Stoven's contacts have to be checked out, Mr Claydon.'

'At the same time . . . well, you can check me! The Group Captain certainly did. But in the end he came back to my conclusion, which is that Shavers is the man you want.'

His gaze was between fearful and indignant, with the shrewd little face tight and twitching. He seemed to be chiding Gently as for an unexpected act of treachery. Then he remembered the cigarette and began to punish it again.

'If I may I'll keep the letter.'

'Please do. You could ring Russell now.'

'At what time did you leave your shop?'

'It is exactly half an hour's drive to Southgate.'

'Then at three-thirty?'

'That's simple arithmetic. And you can ask Elizabeth, who I left in charge.'

'Then you have no more to worry about, Mr Claydon. Either from the Group Captain or myself.'

But Claydon scarcely seemed reassured.

'I have to repeat, that all this is a shock . . . first the accounts, then Hannah, and now accusations from all directions. Thank God my wife knows nothing about it – she thinks I'm out now at a bridge-club committee.'

'She is a total invalid?'

'She never goes out. She had some back trouble several years ago. According to Dr Capel she's as well as she'll ever be, but that's not saying much . . . I don't want her worried.'

Gently knocked out his pipe and rose.

'Now . . . if you've nothing more to tell me . . .'

'I'm sorry. It was Shavers principally . . . I can't let that fellow make a scene at the shop.'

'I'll take care of Shavers.'

'You do understand. A scandal at the shop would be the last straw.'

'I understand.'

Claydon stood tremulously blinking at him, still wanting to linger, to say something.

'I suppose you wouldn't know . . . or you, yourself . . . in the normal way, it's a healthy business. If I could only hold on through this recession . . . by Christmas, even, I'd be back in profit.'

'Are you asking me to lend you money?'

'Could you? I swear it's only a temporary embarrassment. Suddenly, out of the blue, I find I'm liable at the end of the month . . .'

It was pitiful, the more so because clearly he wasn't expecting the bid to succeed, just that it was dragged out of him by a sort of compulsion, like that with which he snatched out a fresh cigarette.

'I'll buy your Suckling.'

'The Suckling, yes – I can let you have it worth the money . . . a fine copy, extra-illustrated . . . a house like this should have one . . .'

'And meanwhile, here's a bit of advice. Don't let Riddlesworth pump you again.'

'No, I'm sorry. But I was feeling guilty . . .'

'And the same applies to reporters.'

He steered Claydon firmly back to the hall and opened the door for him. Outside the moon, now high, was making ghosts of the shrubs and trees. Also there was an owl hooting, somewhere over the heather.

'I left my car outside . . .'

Even now the bookseller wanted to cling. He halted outside on the gravel to puff smoke into the keen air. Finally, with a jerky nod of his head, he set off towards the gates; and shortly afterwards Gently heard a door clunk and a car pull away.

The ridiculous fellow! Yet you couldn't help feeling sorry for him and his apparently genuine troubles. Adding two and two together, they probably included a wife who knew how to keep him under her thumb . . .

He returned to the lounge, collected the phone, and carried it across to a chair by the hearth. But clearly this wasn't going to be his night, because just as he sat, the phone rang.

'Gently here.'

'Chiefie, listen –'

He could have thrown the phone across the room! Out of it, beside Shavers' voice, was coming the tinkle of a piano and a drone of conversation. The ex-con was ringing from the bar of the Eel's Foot, where doubtless he'd been questioning all and sundry: likely, he'd got one or two lined up, all ready to swear to his snowy innocence.

'Get off the line, Shavers!'

'Chiefie, you can't blame me for trying to put myself in the clear –'

'I don't want to know.'

'But I've got a right to do the best I can for myself –'

'Does that include threatening Mr Claydon?'

'Who says I threatened him? Just a friendly little chat was all! And if it comes to that, he's the sort of drip who might have pulled a job like this. His wife's no good to him, did you know that?'

'Never mind his wife – lay off him.'

'Well, if you say so, Chiefie, but I'm not going to take the rap for a little wet like him. Can't you imagine him sniffing round Hannah?'

'I can imagine you far better.'

'Chiefie, how many times have I got to tell you –'

Gently held the phone and the babble towards the hearth.

Yet something he might learn from the anxious ex-con – Riddlesworth, evidently, wasn't letting grass grow under his feet. His call to Claydon might have been the act of an innocent man seeking information . . . but equally that of a guilty man, seeking out the holes he would need to stop. And one of these . . .

'Can you hear me, Chiefie?'

'Shut up, Shavers, and listen to me.'

'But I've got some info –'

'What I want to know is whether Group Captain Riddlesworth has been in touch with you.'

'Well, stone the crows!'

'Has he?'

'He was on the blower an hour ago. Came the bleeding heavy with me, pretending you were just going to pick me up. You aren't, are you?'

'Did you put him on to Moulton?'

'Chiefie, I may look stupid –'

'Is Moulton in the bar?'

'He's here.'

'Get hold of him and put him on.'

Shavers laid down the phone, but Gently could hear his muted voice calling distantly; also a sharp, scolding female voice raised in interrogation. Myrtle . . .

'Hullo – Moulton?'

'That's me . . .'

'Pay attention to what I'm going to tell you. Tomorrow you'll be making a statement to Inspector Leyston, and in the meantime you'll keep your mouth buttoned. Is that understood?'

'But look here, old matey –'

'You'll answer nobody's questions but ours. And that means nobody's. If I hear different, I shall have you picked up straight away.'

Heavy breathing from the other end!

'Right you are . . . I'll do what you say.'

'You'd better.'

'I'll do it . . .'

'Now put Shavers back on.'

The phone changed hands, and there were grumbling words that died away in the sound of the piano.

'Shavers?'

'I'm here, Chiefie . . . you didn't need to be so tough on Ted.'

'From you, I want to know what Riddlesworth was asking.'

'So it is him . . .'

'Just answer the question!'

'All right, all right! It was all about Hannah, how long I'd known her and when we'd met.'

'About names she may have dropped?'

'You must have been listening. Then he wanted my movements, too. Tried to sell me the idea that if I didn't cough up, you'd be round to pinch me before I could blink.'

'And you coughed?'

'Do me a favour. I told him to mind his sodding business. All he got out of me was that he'd better watch his step, never mind mine. But that wasn't why –'

'Moulton's name wasn't mentioned?'

'I'm telling you . . . now can I get a word in? You were on

about a car parked up at the gorses, and that's why I rang you in the first bleeding place.'

Gently shifted his grip. 'A car . . . ?'

'Yes . . . and it wasn't my car, either! Your dozy slop has been talking to Sid Norton, who saw me loading mine down at the yard.'

'So who saw the other car?'

'Chiefie, this isn't a con. It was Bob Gourbold's missus who saw it. They live in a cottage near Bodney church, and yesterday she biked into Thwaite to shop. So she sees this car pulled in at the gorses and thinks maybe it's a couple there having it off. And that was around three p.m., which was when Sid saw me loading up.'

'And the Gourbolds are customers?'

'Have a heart, Chiefie! It was Bob who told me. I haven't talked to Dot.'

'What colour was the car?'

'I didn't ask, did I? You'll have to ask Dot about that.'

Gently stared at the cigarette ash lying on the carpet.

'All right . . . we'll check it out.'

'And I'm in the clear?'

'You're in the clear when I say so.'

'Now Chiefie, you'll have to get off my back some time . . .'

He depressed the studs and rang Leyston. The voice of the local man sounded weary.

'I've been ringing round the camp-sites . . . about half of them have closed down for the season.'

'Any luck?'

'None. The trouble is, he could be anywhere . . .'

Gently gave him a synopsis of events that evening, which probably did little to cheer him up. You didn't need to select the facts to show which way the case was moving.

'If it's Riddlesworth, do you think we'll ever nail him, sir?'

'Even he can't hide his son for ever. And meanwhile we must check and keep checking – we shall need all the answers when we move in.'

'But if the son knows nothing . . .'

'Something he must know, or he wouldn't have vanished so conveniently.'

He hung up and poured himself a drink, seeking a pause before he talked to Gabrielle. All unconscious of his involvements, she sat waiting his ring in distant Rouen. Should he tell her? He sipped deliberately for some moments, then shook his head. Enough that he should be aware of the tragedy that had happened, just a few miles off . . .

'Sorry I'm late. I've been talking to a bookseller about the purchase of a Suckling.'

'A Suckling? What is that?'

'A county history . . . expert opinion is that we should own one.'

'Aha. And how much is he asking?'

'I'm afraid I forgot to enquire.'

Poor Claydon. Now, among his other worries, he would have the burden of dealing with Gabrielle.

7

'What time will your missus be back, Mr George?'

It was the thought that Gently had woken up with: that, in twelve hours' time, he would be standing on a platform, waiting for the train bringing Gabrielle home.

Sunday morning at Heatherings was one of those moments that he was learning to savour, a time of perfect leisure whose signature was the chime of the bells in the village. When they stopped, you could hear a bell more distant, probably that of the church across the Walks; and when, shortly after, that ceased too, Mrs Jarvis would be knocking on the door with the tea tray.

'Expect us at nine . . .'

'Will she want a meal?'

Almost certainly, Gabrielle would. One of the first things Gently had noticed about her was her ready and eager appetite. How she kept her figure was a mystery perhaps known only to the French; it was because, she claimed, that unlike the English she didn't stuff herself at breakfast . . .

'It's going to be a fine day, Mr George.'

He had only to open his eyes to see that. From the windows in their room in the east wing the prospect of the Walks folded away. The heather was dark now, past its prime, but still purplish as it smoked in steady sun; birches that edged it had turned auburn, the distant poplars a delicate yellow.

He sipped his tea and glanced at the papers, as usual thumbing through them from back to front. From the bathroom came the sound of water being run, while below, in the garden, a blackbird was sounding its silly alarm.

A long way from London . . .

Why had he listened to that cajoling Chief Constable and his troubles?

'Your bath is ready, Mr George.'

In a sulky mood he took his bath and afterwards went down to breakfast. Sun was peering through the breakfast-room window and lighting up a corner of the table. It was Sunday for all the world, so why not Sunday for him . . . ? Mrs Jarvis, for instance, was already dressed smartly, and smelling of violets, to go to second service.

'Are you in for lunch today, Mr George?'

'I'll see . . .'

Still chewing it over, he strolled down the garden, noticing that the gardener had pruned the rose bushes and tied up the Michaelmas daisies with orange twine. The martins had left, and only yesterday he had heard the harsh notes of passing fieldfares . . . here, these were the things he wanted to be occupied with, not the guilt and fear of wretched people!

But it wouldn't do. He could feel himself a truant, even in enjoying the fresh, cool air. In the end he strode back to the house and the lounge still smelling of Claydon's cigarettes. He rang the police station.

'Anything fresh?'

He thought he could detect relief in Leyston's voice.

'Yes . . . the colour of the car. It was white. And I've got a couple of fresh statements . . .'

He lit his pipe and went to look for Mrs Jarvis, but she had already left for church. He propped a note for her against the tea-caddy, then locked up and went to fetch his car.

'White, and what else?'

'She said it looked newish, but couldn't remember the make or registration.'

'Which way was it pointing?'

'Towards Harford, as though it had come from the Maltings direction.'

Sun was also flooding Leyston's office, making the shabby furniture look yet shabbier, and seeming to bring out the smell of soot which was always dogging the place.

Below in the street Sunday cars cruised by, looking cleaner

and shinier than on weekdays, and family groups, dressed in their best, strolled without urgency or stopped to chat.

Driving in, Gently had glimpsed a sea that faded into the sky with scarcely a seam, while, at the end of its causeway, the Martello Tower threw a hard, dark shadow.

'She reckons the time at five past three, because three was when she left home, and the car was gone again when she came back, which was between quarter and half past four.'

'She heard nothing?'

'She says not.'

'Through the gap, she might have seen the boats.'

'Says she was staring at the gorse as she rode by, on the chance of catching two of them at it.'

It was tantalising. Everything pointed to the car having been Riddlesworth's, and witness had passed and repassed the spot at times that were probably crucial. If her curiosity had got the better of her or if her observation of the car had been more exact, they would now have had information that the Group Captain couldn't have brushed aside.

As it was, they had nothing that he couldn't outface with a stout denial.

'What were the fresh statements?'

'One is from a Mrs Davies who lives opposite the Maltings. She was outside playing with her children and remembers hearing a car drive away from Riddlesworth's at about two. She didn't see the car because of a high hedge, but heard it come down the drive and turn towards the village.'

'Probably his wife leaving.'

'That's what I thought . . . one of the people I've rung is the vicar. He says Mrs Riddlesworth collected the church key at quarter past two, but he can't say when she returned it because she put it through the letter-box.'

Gently grunted. A chink there?

'What else?'

Leyston picked up a form.

'Mason took this statement from a Frederick Willis, who does a lot of birdwatching on the marsh. He has often seen a sailing dinghy, sailed mostly by a young man, but sometimes by an older man and once by a woman. He has also seen it beached with a motor-dinghy on the opposite bank, but can't say who was with it at the time.'

'"Mostly sailed by a young man" . . .'

'That'd be the son.'

Gently held out his hand for the statement. Like Dot Gourbold's, it came irritatingly close to saying a lot while saying only a little. They knew all of what was down there, yet suddenly the intelligence seemed to come up fresh, as though, through the laboured handwriting, he was seeing it with different eyes.

'Any line on young Riddlesworth?'

'Not yet. He doesn't seem to be staying on a regular campsite.'

'Have you queried the music school?'

'I was going to ring them, only today there may be nobody there.'

'Ring them, and if there is, say we'll be calling on them in half an hour.'

Leyston consulted a well-worn directory, ran his nail along an entry and dialled. Someone answered, and he gave the message, listening for a moment before hanging up.

'They're giving a concert this evening to an invited audience . . . most of the students are in residence, anyway.'

But Gently was still brooding over the statement and scarcely seemed to be listening. At last he passed the statement back to Leyston,

'Have you anything new on Shavers?'

'Just confirmation. Witness saw him and his car at the moorings at about three-thirty. Then there's Moulton's statement . . . which leaves out the bit about him seeing Shavers on his yacht.'

Steps forwards and backwards . . . !

'What colour is his car?'

'It's a beige Cortina estate.'

'Have you checked Claydon's movements?'

'There's confirmation from Russell, but Claydon's manageress has gone out for the day.'

Isolate Riddlesworth, that was the game: close out every other available suspect. Then he would be left alone in the middle, with his assertions growing thinner at each repetition.

And with the son to come . . .

Leyston said: 'Chigwell have been on the phone about Hannah Stoven's ex-husband. Seems he was out photographing a development site on Friday and Chigwell didn't contact him till yesterday. They say he intends to come down here.'

Gently was silent. He had almost forgotten about Hannah's ex-husband! But Stoven was another who would have to be checked off before the ring round Riddlesworth was complete.

'We'll have a word with him when we see him. But our first priority is Mark Riddlesworth.'

'Just thought I ought to mention him.'

In Leyston's sad eyes was a gleam of what might even have been taken for pleasure.

Though it was barely mid-morning the car park at the Maltings was already filling up, and visitors were strolling about the grassy frontage or straying along a rough path beside the river. Of the mist there was no sign: the still, bright sun had rolled it up. Sun sparkled on the river, which was at half-flood, and gave a reddish tone to its fringe of dead reeds. Buildings were sharp in light and shade, with a sheen on their slate roofs. The craft shop was open, and in the concert hall forecourt a display of vintage cars formed a lively attraction.

A fine Sunday in October: an Indian summer. There were even late swallows to skim the river . . .

'Look over there, sir.'

They had parked under willows from which yellow leaves were dropping on the cars. Across at the quay, a stocky figure had turned to watch their arrival. Today Riddlesworth was dressed in quiet tweeds, which, on him, seemed almost a disguise; he made no attempt to hide his interest, but stood boldly staring at the two policemen.

'Shall we have a word with him?'

'Not yet.'

Gently glanced round the cars on the park. Only half a dozen places from their own stood a glinting white Jaguar XJS-HE. Deliberately, he walked across to it and sauntered round the expensive car: then paused to stare at Riddlesworth, who stared back without a flicker of expression.

A moment of challenge!

And each of them knew it, standing there in the soft sun, with visitors strolling between them and a car creeping by, looking for a space. They were suddenly alone, the two of them, aware that battle had been joined.

'Let's go.'

Gently turned away casually, pausing at his own car to lock the door. He didn't look back, though Leyston could scarcely tear his eyes away from Riddlesworth.

'Shouldn't we tackle him about the car?'

Gently shook his head. What was the use? They didn't hold enough cards in their hand – yet! Later on, when they were holding trumps . . .

A board directed them to the music school, which was housed in buildings behind the concert hall. They pushed open swing doors to be met by a barrage of musical discord from somewhere within. But just at that moment a voice barked sharply and the discord tailed away, to be replaced, after a short pause, by a slow, controlled succession of phrases.

'Are you the policemen?'

A head had poked round a door in the hall they had entered, that of a bland-faced woman wearing glasses, with hair braided tightly on the top of her head.

'Am I speaking to a tutor?'

The woman laughed. 'I'm Sheila, the dogsbody who runs the office. Did you want to see a tutor?'

'I'd like a few words with the tutor responsible for Mark Riddlesworth.'

'Oh dear. Is Mark in trouble?'

'Just that he may be able to help us.'

The woman stared at him uncertainly, as though trying to make up her mind what to do. Tall and lean, she was wearing a dress in flowered material that reached to her ankles.

'You see there's only Geoffrey here, and he's busy with a rehearsal . . . he'll be livid if we interrupt. But they'll be breaking for coffee in half an hour.'

'Is he Mark's tutor?'

'He's one of them, yes. Adrian takes Mark in musical theory.'

'Perhaps Geoffrey wouldn't mind breaking half an hour early.'

'Well . . . I'll see. But if he bites your head off . . .'

She led them down the hall to double doors from behind which the music was emanating, and timidly pushed them open: just as a bassoon gave a hoarse warble.

'Get out, damn you!'

'I'm sorry, Geoffrey . . .'

She slipped aside hastily to let them enter. In a large, high room young men and girls were seated in a semicircle, each with an instrument. On a rostrum before them stood a plump, bearded man, who had turned an angry face towards the door. He was dressed in a turtle-neck sweater and held a baton which he raised threateningly. Meanwhile the music had faded to silence.

'Sheila, you know the rules of this place.'

'I'm sorry Geoffrey, but these gentlemen —'

'I don't give a hoot for any gentlemen!'

'They're policemen.'

'And I'm a conductor — and I've got a performance to give tonight.'

But after a few more testy growls he threw down the baton and bawled that the orchestra would take a break. Immediately there was a stir and a scrape of chairs, then a rush of feet towards the exit. The plump man came over.

'So what do you fellows want?'

'Perhaps we can talk about it in your office.'

'It's about that bloody woman, is it?'

'Were you expecting us?'

'Why not, when she came ashore at our doorstep?'

Grudgingly, he led them to another room where there were comfortable armchairs. It was probably his den, and besides shelves of books contained a piano and music deck. It had a window facing the bend of the river and smelled of pipe-smoke and beer.

'Fetch us some coffee, Sheila.'

He prowled round the room, to come up with a pipe. A large teddy-bear of a man, his beard was greying and his hair thinning on top. In the sweater his big body looked shapeless, while the rolled collar gave him a neckless appearance.

'Who am I talking to, by the way?'

Gently told him.

'I'm Geoffrey Waterhouse. I run this school and produce musicians.'

'I am told that Mark Riddlesworth is one of your students.'

'What do you want to know about him?'

'What sort of a student is he?'

'He wants to be a composer, which makes it lucky that he has money and influence behind him.'

'Is he a talented young man?'

'Just now he's working on a song cycle based on traditional airs – the usual two-finger exercise for budding composers. What is your interest in him anyway?'

He had dropped into one of the armchairs, to sit regarding Gently with narrowed eyes. Sheila brought the coffee. Waterhouse sipped his with the pipe still hanging from the corner of his mouth.

'Is he a popular student?'

'He isn't unpopular. In looks, he takes after his mother – slim, fine-featured, fair hair worn with a quiff. Shy with girls, though I doubt if that means much. He's no great mixer with either sex.'

'No girl friend then.'

'None that I know of.'

'How about men?'

'He makes a pal of Rick Woodward – a flautist with real prospects, who doesn't mind helping him with his arranging.'

'Is Woodward in today?'

'He's playing a solo in the concert tonight.'

'I would like to talk to him.'

Waterhouse stared for a while, then raised his head to shout:

'Rick!'

They were joined by a dark-haired, moustached youngster, who entered without knocking. He glanced questioningly at Waterhouse before venturing a look at the other two men.

'Rick, these gentlemen are policemen, and that one there is top brass. For reasons completely obscure he wants to ask you questions about Mark Riddlesworth.'

'About Mark . . . ?'

'Exactly, child. No need for you to be coy.'

'But . . . I haven't seen him since Friday.'

'Tell him, fool. Not me.'

Woodward faced Gently doubtfully.

'Sir, I don't really know Mark very well . . .'

Gently sipped coffee before asking: 'How long have you and he been acquainted?'

'Well . . . since autumn term last year. But we've never been close friends. Just that we're interested in the same things . . . and I happen to think his music is rather good.'

'So you are often in his company.'

'Yes, I suppose so. Though we don't live in each other's pockets.'

'For example, have you ever been camping with him?'

'Actually, once. But camping isn't my thing.'

'Tell me about it.'

Woodward was getting flustered; he sent an appealing look to Waterhouse. A smooth-skinned youth, his dark bar of moustache gave him a faintly Latin appearance.

'Well . . . Mark is keen on cycle-camping, and once he invited me to join him. I borrowed a sleeping-bag from one of the fellows and we cycled up the coast. But it wasn't a success. The tent got full of sand, and I never slept a wink.'

'Which site did you camp on?'

'We camped on the beach . . . at night, the sand gets as cold as marble.'

'Which beach was that?'

'At Grimchurch, about half a mile from the village.'

'Has he ever spoken of other places he has been to?'

'If he has, I don't remember.'

'Perhaps after a longer trip than usual?'

Woodward thought about it, but shook his head. 'After I had tried it I lost interest . . . I suppose I'm not a very enterprising type. Mark is used to roughing it, but that night on the beach was the very end.'

He looked half-ashamed of himself, as though somehow it reflected on his manhood. Waterhouse was nursing his pipe and gazing at the ceiling with a long-suffering expression.

'Did you ever go sailing with him?'

'That was the same. I went for one trip in his dinghy. But it was pretty cramped and boring, and he would never let me take the helm.'

'Where did you go?'

'Down to Bodney church, and then we explored one of the creeks. Mark was bothering about the tide all the time, afraid we wouldn't get back.'

'Did you meet other boats?'

'No.'

'Did you see any moored to the bank?'

'It was April and pretty cold, I remember that. It must have been before other boats were about.'

'Did he suggest mooring anywhere?'

'We had brought a thermos and sandwiches, and pulled up on the bank for lunch. That was at a spot not far from the church, but it was freezing cold. We didn't linger.'

'Was Mark expecting to meet someone there?'

Woodward looked surprised. 'No, he wasn't.'

'A girl friend, perhaps?'

'Mark doesn't have one . . . at least, I've never heard him mention her.' He flushed suddenly. 'I say! Is this to do with what's been happening . . . ?'

'Moron!' Waterhouse growled round his pipe.

Woodward looked thoroughly put out. His colour came and went and he shifted from one foot to the other. He blurted:

'Well, all I can say is, *I* don't know anything about it! And I'm certain that Mark doesn't either, and – and that's all I've got to say.'

'You last saw him on Friday?'

'I don't know! Yes, all right. Friday morning.'

'Not later than that?'

'Because after lunch I was rehearsing, while Mark was probably doing theory.'

'Thank you, Mr Woodward.'

'But I'd just like to say –'

'Bugger off young Woodward!' Waterhouse growled.

Woodward hung on briefly, his eyes large, then he turned and left in haste.

Waterhouse noisily sucked coffee. 'It's an education,' he said. 'But now you've finished turning young Rick inside out, perhaps you can tell me what it's about.'

Gently shrugged. 'On Friday, what time did classes finish here?'

'At four-thirty.'

'It was four-thirty when Mark Riddlesworth left this building?'

'Well . . . it should have been.'

'How is that?'

Waterhouse drew on his pipe, scowling. 'I suppose I shall have to tell you, to stop you grilling the entire establishment! The fact is, he didn't turn up after lunch. He was due for sessions with Adrian and with me, then he should have attended an evening rehearsal, because, damn him, he was down to play tonight.'

'He was absent from the lunch break onwards?'

'So what?'

Gently paused. 'Was that perhaps something that had happened before?'

Waterhouse chewed on the pipe-stem. 'All right! You have to expect students to play hookey sometimes. Mark is no worse than the rest. And he's always contrite about it afterwards.'

'How often has it happened?'

'I don't keep a record.'

'Once a week? Once a fortnight?'

'Damn it, not so often.'

'When did it start?'

'He was punctual enough till the sailing season.'

'It began, say, in April?'

'I can't give you a date.'

'But his absences were always in the afternoon?'

'Stop badgering me, blast you! Anyone would think I'd done for the bloody woman myself.' Waterhouse stared fiercely, his brows ridging. 'There's no mystery about it, anyway. The kid's keen on sailing and birdwatching, and that's why it started when it did. And I daresay the tides were a factor.'

'Yes – the tides.'

'An afternoon with a flood slack would be irresistible. He could scull around in the creeks and get back before the ebb had him in trouble.'

'In short, from April there was a pattern of truancy, always in the afternoons, and probably linked to the tides.'

Waterhouse said bitterly: 'That's what you're getting me to say, and a lot of good may it do you.'

'Do *you* know where Mark has gone, Mr Waterhouse?'

'No, I don't. And now it's time I got back to rehearsals.'

He heaved his large body out of the armchair and stood waiting, scowling, for them to leave. He reminded one of some fierce animal, who, nevertheless, might let children cuddle him.

'Don't be too clever – that's my advice. I know Mark and you don't.'

'If Mark turns up here, please ring us.'

'I may – if I've nothing better to do.'

He stalked away to the rehearsal-room, from which a fresh

medley of discord was proceeding. Once more, his bawl produced silence, and, after an interval, sweet harmony.

Riddlesworth's car was still on the park, and now had its owner standing beside it. He was being made the target of a harangue by a meagre, bushy-haired man, dressed in a black suit and tie. Leyston murmured:

'That's her father . . . I remember him from the Festival.'

As he talked, Stefan Makovrilov was gesturing with pale, corpse-like hands. He had impish, expressive features and glittering dark eyes; words poured from him excitedly, in contrast to the jerked responses of Riddlesworth.

'What do you reckon he's on about?'

Gently's shoulders twitched. 'Probably he just wants to talk.'

Riddlesworth's face told him nothing, so he kept his eyes on the musician's. A tired face, in spite of its animation: the man had probably been travelling all night, taking a sleeper down from Edinburgh, but finding anything but sleep as he tossed in his berth. And now, on a bright English Sunday, among people at leisure who knew or cared nothing . . . While, down the bank – had he seen it? – her dinghy still lay, unclaimed.

'He's looking this way, sir.'

A hand on Makovrilov's arm, Riddlesworth was nodding towards the two policemen; then he paused for a moment, eyeing them, before getting in his car and starting the engine. The white car idled by them almost insolently, and at less than walking speed, before swinging in a slow turn towards the yard and the road.

Meanwhile Makovrilov had joined them.

'I am Hannah Stoven's father . . . are you not the policemen who seek her assassin? Very good! I require the key of my daughter's residence in Shinglebourne.'

'The key, sir?'

'Yes, the key. I wish to visit the place where she lived. Have no fear, I am next of kin, and all that is there belonged to Hannah.'

'Well, I don't know, sir,' Leyston demurred. 'Not at this stage of the investigation.'

'But I am her father!'

'I'm sorry, sir. But I don't think we can do that.'

'Listen, listen . . . I want her key!'

Wretchedly, it seemed he might burst into tears. His mouth was drooped and quivering helplessly, and his glittering eyes over-brilliant.

'Give him the key.'

'I shouldn't, sir . . .'

'Stretch a point, and give him the key.'

Reluctantly Leyston felt in his pocket and brought out a tagged key. Makovrilov grasped it eagerly.

'It comes back to the police station,' Gently said.

'Yes, I promise . . . the police station.' He swallowed hard. 'Where is my daughter?'

'At Ipswich. But there may be some delay in securing a release.'

They watched him drive off in a blue Escort which bore the plate of a local hire firm, and almost at once a patrol car came bumping urgently across the yard.

'Message from the station for you, sir. They've got a Mr Stoven there, waiting to see you.'

Gently grimaced. One way or another, Sunday was going to be a day for relatives . . .

8

'I am the dead woman's ex-husband, and I came as soon as I could after hearing the dreadful news. I realise, naturally, that in my position I must be under immediate suspicion.'

'Take a chair, Mr Stoven.'

'I want to say at once that I know nothing whatever about what has happened.'

'Please sit down . . .'

'Entirely by accident, I am unable to prove my movements on Friday beyond doubt.'

Gently sighed, and automatically took Leyston's chair behind the desk. He knew the feel of it; three years ago he had interrogated other suspects in that office. Then it had been in the enervating heat of a summer that had gone on for too long, with the ancient fan that stood in the corner wheezing and groaning ineffectively. Another case, other suspects; but the scene itself had barely changed.

'Were you by any chance in this district on Friday?'

'No, of course not – nowhere near! Only since I was working on my own, I don't see how I can prove it. I was to have met the representative of a development firm, but for some reason he failed to turn up. On the other hand, I do have these photographs to show you . . .'

Dennis Stoven was about forty, and he had brought with him a fat briefcase. If he was nervous, it was probably only the nervousness of a man finding himself caught in an awkward situation. He was dressed primly in a sober lounge suit and a discreetly-striped shirt with sharp collar and tie. His hair was worn short, and he had the pallid, unsmiling features that one associated with lawyers' clerks or council officials.

Yet he was an interesting man: because what had it been

about him that had persuaded Hannah to take him for a husband?

'Where were you, then?'

'At Curate's Green. That's a development site near Colchester. The original developers went broke and work stopped on the site six months ago. I was employed to make a preliminary survey by the firm who are negotiating to take it over – Newgate Holdings. They will certainly confirm that I was sent there on Friday.'

'But their representative didn't arrive.'

'I've already admitted that. However, it didn't affect what I'd gone there to do. Perhaps you may care to look at these photographs . . .'

He spread them on the desk, a bunch of black-and-white glossies showing houses in different states of completion, also unmade-up roads and a builder's compound stocked with bricks, timber and breeze blocks.

'What do these prove?'

'Well, at least I was there, and made a preliminary survey of the development.'

'These photographs could have been taken at any time.'

'I couldn't have known that Newgate's man wasn't going to turn up.'

Gently fingered the photographs. The truth was that he felt scarcely any suspicions about Stoven – had expected him to produce a solid alibi and satisfactorily phase himself out of the enquiry. And now the foolish fellow had gone out of his way to establish the precise contrary: as though he wanted to get in on the action! Surely he could furnish proof of some sort?

'How long were you there?'

'My appointment was for ten, and I remained on the site till five.'

'Did you pick up a key?'

'That wasn't necessary.'

'Where did you have lunch?'

'I brought some sandwiches with me.'

'And you saw absolutely no one?'

'The site is isolated, two miles away from the village.'

'Weren't there any kids playing around it?'

'I'm afraid not.'

'Perhaps a tractor in the fields?'

'The harvest is over.'

It was a model of a non-alibi, wellnigh as foolproof as Riddlesworth's. The difference was that, in Stoven's case, you could almost swear that it was true.

'What colour is your car?'

'A white Renault 18, but I'm afraid there's nothing distinctive about it.'

'How old?'

'I took delivery in August, when the new date-letter was due.'

You could hardly believe it. It was one of those coincidences sent to plague the life of the police. Grumpily, Gently shuffled the photographs together and handed them back to Stoven. Had there been a scintilla of evidence against this man he'd have come to hand like a pint pot . . .

'Exactly what was your position with regard to the dead woman?'

'Well, I can't conceal that I paid her an allowance. I suppose you'll think that's against me, but I was perfectly able and willing to pay it. I bore Hannah no grudge. We parted amicably, and she still regarded me as a friend. I made the Tower over to her entirely. She was fond of Shinglebourne because of its musical associations.'

He spoke of her with no emotion, but was probably of a type to have concealed it anyway. What was intriguing was that he had actually lived with her and was speaking of her, as it were, from the inside. All the others had seen her from the outside, finding her more or less of an enigma.

'How did you meet her?'

'She worked for the partnership . . . she had been through business school, you know. I was the junior partner and she worked in my office, doing secretarial jobs. Her English was sometimes quaint, but she was capable for all that.'

'What attracted you to her?'

He paused over that one. 'I suppose, because at that time I was interested in music. She often had tickets for concerts when her father was performing in town.'

'You married her for that – a joint interest in music?'

'No . . . it wasn't only that!'

'Then why?'

Stoven stiffened slightly, his humourless face resenting.

'I don't really see what that has to do with it, but I suppose you have some purpose in asking these questions. No doubt I married Hannah because I was in love with her, and believed that she was in love with me.'

In a sudden inspiration, Gently asked: 'Was she your first woman?'

'Really! I don't feel called upon –'

'Was she?'

'Well, you could say that . . .'

'How old were you then?'

'. . . Thirty.'

It fitted. He was timid with women, and perhaps teetering on the brink of resigned bachelorhood: sexually, a lame duck, the type to whom Hannah instinctively responded. Why? A response, it might be, from the depths of her own alien-ness, a tenderness towards another lost soul, a reaching out to touch hands. She, who had been torn from her roots so brutally, so young, had a keen eye for a human casualty.

'Who was it suggested marriage?'

'If you must know . . . Hannah.'

Yes.

'Were you living together at the time?'

He scarcely needed to ask that question!

'It isn't what you think . . . my lease ran out, and I was desperate to find another flat. Hannah had a flat not far from the office and she suggested that, for the time being . . .'

'How soon were you married?'

'A year later.'

'How long did it last?'

'Five years.'

'What broke it up?'

'I don't know, it's difficult to explain! But it wasn't because . . .'

Not because he was impotent, he'd been about to say. Gently eyed him with a grain of pity. He must have feared it, and she had probably understood his fears, making her response to him yet stronger. But it wasn't because . . .

Stoven was missing his eye and spots of colour had appeared in his cheeks.

'Your interest in music lapsed.'

'Well, I suppose . . . my work made extra demands on me. But we still went to concerts together, at least when her father was in town. But it wasn't that either. I can't explain . . . if I told you what happened, you'd never believe me. Sometimes I felt like a child at school who had passed an exam, after which it was expected . . .'

A child at school!

'Let me guess. Hannah introduced you to another woman.'

'How . . . how could you know that?'

'One day, you had a serious talk together.'

'Yes – exactly! But how could you guess?'

'And that woman is now your wife?'

'Mary, yes – I know it sounds preposterous, but that's exactly how it happened . . .'

His stare was now astonished, now doubting, as though he couldn't decide whether Gently was being serious.

'Mary – she was a draughtswoman whom Hannah had met at the office . . . she had a boy friend at one time, but for some reason they broke up. Hannah took to inviting her out with us . . . honestly, it was none of my doing! At the time, I just looked on Mary as a friend. Then suddenly, it was as though we had always planned it that way . . .'

'You were still sleeping with Hannah?'

'Yes, until . . .'

'Had Hannah ever thought she might be pregnant?'

'No, we had given up expecting . . .'

Spots were showing in his cheeks again.

'She more or less arranged things. We didn't even have lawyers . . . if everything is agreed, it seems you don't need them. I made over the Tower to her, and she suggested an allowance much less than I was ready to give her. I swear there was no ill-feeling at all. She simply opted out and gave place to Mary.'

'No suggestion that Hannah had a boy friend.'

'No – believe me!'

'Either at that end – or this?'

Stoven gazed, then shook his head. 'We knew some people here, but not very well.'

'Who did you know?'

'We belonged to the yacht club. We got to know a few members and officials.'

'For example, a past-commodore?'

'If you mean Group Captain Riddlesworth, yes, we knew him fairly well. He was interested in the conversion we were doing – the Tower was just a shell when we leased it from the council.'

'He was friendly with Hannah?'

'There was nothing like that . . .'

'Has she ever mentioned him to you, since?'

'Yes, once or twice! We exchanged letters and cards, though I haven't actually seen her since we parted. But nothing that might lead one to expect . . .'

'In May, Hannah had a pregnancy test. Did she make any mention of that?'

'Good heavens . . . no!'

'Or of any boy friend?'

'Absolutely none.'

But he looked shaken. Perhaps, for the first time, what had happened was seeming real. Behind the stark fact of Hannah's death there had been circumstances, people . . .

'Surely, you can't suspect . . . ?'

'Hannah died at a rendezvous with a lover.'

117

'Oh my God . . . the poor girl. How could anyone do such a thing?'

'Perhaps from jealousy. Or a different motive.'

'But I don't see how one could be jealous of Hannah. She was so kind . . . the last person in the world to have provoked an act of violence.'

'Yet, if she had stood in someone's way?'

He paled slightly, and sat very still.

'Is that the idea, then – that I might have done it to save paying out her allowance?'

Was it the idea? Gently had made a pass with it almost as an act of politeness, just to let Stoven know that he had a stake in the case, wasn't being left out in the cold! But in fact he had already made up his mind. Stoven's only claim was his non-alibi . . .

'You say you made over the Tower to her?'

'Yes. So she wasn't keeping me out of that. I assume that now it will go to her father . . . though if I could, I would like to see it again.'

'Then now is your chance. Her father is down there. You had better get along before he locks up.'

'You mean . . . I can go?'

'Why not? And many thanks for presenting yourself here today.'

Stoven stared, and then rose. But somehow it must have seemed too much like a brush-off. At the door he hesitated, looking back doubtfully at Gently.

'The funeral . . . I want to take care of that. I would like to take Hannah home.'

'You had better discuss that with her father. He may have his own ideas.'

'But we lived together for six years. I'm sure it's what she would have wanted. If I'm willing to pay all the expenses, I don't see why . . .'

'Hannah's father is the next of kin.'

He went, and a little later they saw him set out down the street with reluctant steps; it may have been that he didn't get on too well with Makovrilov and was half-hoping that Gently would hold his hand.

'So where does that get us, sir?'

Gently grunted and felt for his pipe. Mostly where it had got him was a few steps closer to the secret life of Hannah Stoven. For all they knew, there were several alternatives that might fit the circumstances of the crime, but one only that would fit Hannah Stoven, matching her character at all points. Know her, and the rest would fill in. Yet didn't he already know her well enough? He had dismissed Stoven practically out of hand, non-alibi, white car and all . . .

'Think I'll get along to the Tower too, sir. I'm not too happy about letting out the key.'

'Are you afraid they may come to blows?'

Leyston said stolidly: 'I'd sooner that Stoven had accounted for his movements.'

Still that lazy Sunday was unfolding as they drove along the causeway, bright sun, pale sky, no breeze and a sea almost without motion. The bright stillness seemed like a frame enclosing some moments out of time, a picture in which nothing could happen, a sudden shift to a Sunday of childhood. They passed Stoven, now striding out, and the cars of the anglers, the latter stationed along the shingle at precise intervals, each with a rod at the same angle. Did they ever catch anything? Like the sea they seemed to be sleeping at their posts, while down the river a wrinkled sail stood rooted above its reflection. The Tower had its shadow towards them and cut a dark notch in the sky. Beyond it, the spit stretched sunnily, dunes of marram where no shadow was.

'There's Makovrilov's car.'

They parked beside it on a piece of rough ground free from shingle. Across the drawbridge the door stood open, and immediately on entering one smelt cigarette smoke. Claydon . . . ! He was squatting on a stool beside the kneeling form of the musician, who had around him a scatter of papers from a drawer in his daughter's bureau.

'What are you doing here?'

'What ... ? I happen to be acquainted with Mr Makovrilov!'

'He brought you here?'

'I met him . . . I'd come this way for a stroll.'

Claydon was quivering at once, eyes big and indignant behind the glasses. He was dressed this morning in an open-necked shirt that revealed a scrawny though hairy chest.

'I thought . . . it was a mark of respect, just a few quiet moments here. It isn't out of bounds, is it? And then Mr Makovrilov drove up.'

'He is here with permission, but you are not.'

'But I know him very well. He invited me in.'

And suddenly he was looking so wretched that Gently merely shrugged, and turned to the musician.

'Mr Makovrilov?'

'Wait – wait!'

His bushy head was bent over an exercise book. Looking over his shoulder, one could see writing in Hannah Stoven's wispy scribble.

'What have you there?'

'This is important – it is her diary, written in Czech.'

'Her diary!'

'Just so. And it mentions a man . . . I am reading . . .'

His queer, squeezed face was intent, his glinting eyes racing over the page. Then he turned a leaf, but there was no more writing, and he slapped the book shut with a groan.

'This is no good – no good at all. My daughter is always so poetical! But she had a lover, is it not so, who she used to meet on the bank of the river?'

'Is that in her diary?'

'Yes, yes, but I have heard about it before.'

'Heard about it from whom?'

'The Group Captain told me – he has offered to point out the very spot. Only the name you do not know, isn't that right? He cannot tell me, nor Mr Claydon.'

'The Group Captain offered to point out the spot?'

'I tell you yes – do the police not know it? But Mr Claydon tells me about this fisherman who saw Hannah's boat there, and beside it the boat of her lover. So you are searching for him, yes? You have a clue? It is this man who assassinates Hannah? I am her father who is asking you this, who implores justice for his murdered child!'

He had got up from his knees now and begun making vehement gestures at Gently. Leyston was peering at him distastefully while, on his stool, Claydon puffed rapidly.

'Her mother is dead, she is my only child . . .'

'What exactly does she say in her diary?'

'It is what we know, that she has a lover and goes out to meet him in her boat. But my child was a poet . . .'

'Doesn't she name him?'

Makovrilov's hands went to his head. 'Am I not telling you? She has romantic ideas, calling nothing by its proper name. She calls him Endymion.'

'Endymion?'

'You do not know? The shepherd prince? And she visits him according to the moon – which is to say, when the tide is right. So what is that? Have you shepherd princes – is it some farmer keeping sheep?'

'Endymion was a youth . . .'

'Young, old, there is nothing in her diary about that. She goes to meet him in her scallop, and he is wafted to her in his. Then they have dreams, and their farewells are softly called across the waters. This is so, it is what she writes. If you wish, I will translate.'

'What period does it cover?'

Makovrilov snatched up the book.

'In September thirtieth is the last entry. April twenty-eighth it begins. And all is written in the same style.'

'And this is the only one?'

'Look for yourself. The rest is poetry, notes and letters from me. Poor Hannah . . . she is making a romance of everything . . . and in the end . . .'

He covered his face.

'I . . . I told him what I knew,' Claydon stammered. 'I couldn't see any harm.'

'What you knew, or what you suspected?'

'Honestly, I didn't mention any names . . .'

He seemed almost as upset as the musician, and kept blinking at the furniture, especially the books. Catching Gently's eye on him, he nodded to the latter:

'I sold her most of those . . . at cost, of course.'

Meanwhile there were steps on the drawbridge and Stoven entered the room. He paused an instant to glance about him, then hastened to take Makovrilov's arm.

'Stefan.'

'Ach . . . Dennis!'

Makovrilov clasped the architect to him. For a moment it seemed he might kiss his cheeks, but Stoven drew back just in time.

'I came down as soon as I was able. I thought there should be someone here to take charge.'

'Dennis . . . why did you let her go?'

'She wouldn't stay, Stefan.'

'Ach, to meet again . . . here . . . and now!'

Clearly Stoven was finding this awkward, and he gently released himself from the other's embrace. Makovrilov stared at him mistily, then let his hands drop to his sides.

'Had you not heard from her lately, Dennis?'

'She wrote me a letter two months ago.'

'You know she had a lover?'

'So I have been told.'

'She did not speak to you of this?'

Stoven shook his head.

'But is that not strange?' In Makovrilov's tone was a trace of sharpness. 'You talk to each other of these things, yes, they are freely discussed between you?'

'I . . . would have expected her to tell me.'

'Yet she does not?'

'What she wrote about was the Festival. You have seen her

yourself since then, Stefan – at least, she said she expected you down here.'

'The Festival . . . yes.' He dropped his gaze. 'And that was the last time, Dennis. Here, in this room, is where I parted from her . . . here, on this very spot.'

'She didn't mention to you . . .' Stoven began, but the musician was no longer paying him attention. His mouth trembling, he was staring at the carpet, a wild look in his hazed eyes.

'Oh Lord,' Claydon moaned. 'If I'd known, I wouldn't have come in.'

Stoven seemed to notice him for the first time, and turned to frown at the shrinking bookseller.

'Yes, Stan – why *are* you here?'

Claydon goggled up at him. 'I – I met *him*. He looked upset . . . I don't know! And I wanted to see . . . just once . . .'

'What do you know about this?'

'Me!'

'Well, you must have seen as much of her as anyone.'

Claydon's mouth twisted. 'You too. As though it wasn't enough that everyone else . . .' Then he fired up. 'I'll tell you what I know! Hannah has left me in a mess I shall never get out of. At the end of the month, you'll see. I shall be a done man, after that.'

'That's utter rubbish.'

'I haven't slept all night, trying to work out what she's done with the books. But it's the VAT that's going to finish me – where can I find up another five thousand?'

'What had she to do with that?'

'She didn't warn me! It's been mounting up since before the Festival. What I need is help.' He puffed furiously. 'And I can't see why her connections . . .'

'Have you been trying to touch Stefan?'

'No! But where else am I going to turn?'

'And this is all you can think about?'

'You don't understand. I was fond of her too, more than some people.'

'But now you want to soak her relatives.'

'Oh Lord, I need help. Perhaps I'd be better off dead too.'

'I think you are despicable.'

'If you only knew . . .'

'I never liked the idea of her working for you.'

Claydon groaned and squirmed on the stool, but his dominating habit proved too strong for him: stained fingers jerked up a fresh cigarette, though they trembled so much that he could scarcely light up.

Stoven watched him with disgust. In his neatness, his dryness, was a touch of felinity.

'Anyway, you should know something about it. You've been seeing her mostly every day.'

'You've no right to say that! All I know I've told to the Superintendent here.'

'I suppose *you* weren't the boy friend?'

'That's contemptible!'

'And of course, she didn't tell you who he was.'

Jacking himself upright, Claydon spat: 'And I notice she didn't tell you, either.'

'I haven't been seeing her . . .'

'You corresponded.'

'That isn't quite the same thing . . .'

'It would be if she'd still thought anything of you – if she hadn't thrown you on the dust-heap.'

'Now you're being contemptible!'

'Hannah had done with you.'

'At least, she wasn't murdered when she worked for me.'

Sudden electricity! They were glaring at each other, Claydon's magnified eyes wide with hostility. Stoven, on the other hand, looked slightly shocked, like a cat who has found a mouse turning on him.

And all the while, Makovrilov stood motionless, his eyes fixed on that spot on the carpet.

At last Claydon's stare faltered.

'I didn't quite mean all that, you know . .'

'It's all the same if you did.'

'I'm sorry . . . I'm under stress.'

'Do you think it's any better for me?'

'No. But one thing and another . . . I haven't slept, and this place . . . Honestly, I don't know where to turn.'

The fight had ebbed out of him again; he groaned, and applied to his cigarette. Stoven sniffed, but stayed silent. Nevertheless, his eyes were mean. He turned his back and took some steps about the room, pretending to examine Hannah's little arrangements.

Then Makovrilov came out of his trance with some guttural exclamation in Czech. He stormed up to Gently and, drawing himself tall, made jerky gestures before the latter's face.

'Why? Why are you waiting here? Why are you not catching this killer of my child? Is there no law? Am I helpless? Is it like this because we are foreigners?'

'Be assured we are taking every step.'

'Hannah – look – this is Hannah!' He caught up a photograph and shoved it under Gently's nose. 'This is my child – my only child – the little girl they placed in my arms, at the same time telling me my wife is dead. Have you no pity in this country?'

'Oh, my goodness!' Claydon gulped.

'She is a fine girl – a beautiful girl. What does she do to deserve that some Englishman shall take her life away?' He babbled in Czech. 'And it is six weeks – her kisses on my cheeks as I go to my car . . . and now, no more! In your laboratory she is, and soon – down there, down there, under so much earth. I will go with her. I will not stay here in this cruel country of yours. There is no justice, no pity. And here I brought her from the land she loved . . .'

His tirade rambled into Czech again, and then was choked with sobs. He threw himself down on a settee and lay weeping into his hands.

Claydon too had covered his face. Stoven was looking pale

and uncomfortable. Fiddling with a book he'd picked up, he murmured:

'Stefan has always been emotional . . .'

'You had better take care of him.'

'Yes . . .'

'The Inspector wishes to lock up again.'

'I'll get him away.'

But for the moment he didn't seem quite to know how to handle the assignment.

Leyston said: 'Shall we take the diary, sir?'

'I doubt if it can be much help to us.'

All the same, Leyston picked it up and pored over it before dropping it in the bureau drawer.

Finally, Stoven ventured to lay his hand on Makovrilov's shoulder.

'Stefan, we have to go . . .'

'I will stay here! I wish to die where, it is two days, my child is alive.'

'They are going to lock up.'

'Then lock me up! Here is my corner, here is my country. Here I will stay with Hannah.'

But in the end Stoven prevailed.

To Claydon, Gently said: 'Can we give you a lift?'

The little bookseller looked utterly miserable. He no longer had a cigarette and was having to wipe his eyes and glasses.

'That was terrible . . . I never guessed. Do you think he will be all right?'

'Stoven will keep an eye on him.'

'Why do these things happen?' ·

Gently shrugged and motioned him towards the car.

When they had dropped him off they sat for a space in the car in a street which the lunch hour was emptying. Then Leyston said gloomily:

'No doubt about it now, sir. We've got to get our hands on that boy.'

'He was her lover.'

'Yes sir. And it was his old man with the car.'
'It lies between them . . .'
So get the boy; then they could play off one against the other.

9

Later on, Gently was to wonder if things would have turned out differently if, at that juncture, he had left Leyston to get on with it. He felt tempted; and not so much this time because the case was falling together, but more because, heavy within him, he felt a depression about the whole business.

Makovrilov was no doubt one cause of it, with his outbreaks of impassioned grief, and along with these the ex-husband's egoistic attitude and Claydon's mixture of anguish. But was it only that? Didn't it go deeper, finding roots in the character of Hannah herself: Hannah who, could it be, he was coming to know *too* well? Too well . . . ! So that he didn't want to go on with it, tracing her at last to that moment of violence, whether at the hands of son or father: suddenly, he didn't want to know. It was the last of the veils hiding her nakedness, the veils he'd been stripping away at every opportunity; but now it had gone far enough and he would sooner turn away his eyes. Leave her: leave her in her tower, the sad romantic, echoing a myth . . .

But if fate was hanging on that vacillation, it was lunch at the White Hart that settled the matter. When Gently arrived there, the first thing his eye fell on was Riddlesworth's Jaguar, parked out front. Nor was it the only car he recognised. Not far away stood Capel's dusty Volvo. Then there was the rented Escort, alongside a muddy white Renault 18. But it was the Jaguar that renewed the challenge, standing there so gleaming and obviously new. Because wouldn't Riddlesworth have guessed that Gently would come to the White Hart where, on Sundays, lunch was a Shinglebourne institution?

He went into the dining-room, to find Capel occupying a corner table. The doctor was on the watch and at once waved him over.

'If you want a seat, you'd better join me . . . I was hoping you might walk in.'

'Are you on your own?'

'Leslie's on call, and Tanya is visiting her mother.'

Gently sat, at the same time letting his eyes wander round the room. The Riddlesworths had a table at the other end where they sat with heads bowed in conversation. Makovrilov, Stoven and Claydon were sitting near the bar; the musician was conducting himself in a monologue. Stoven was listening with an air of polite boredom, Claydon slumped over a pint, a cigarette trailing.

'A drink?'

'A lager, please.'

As always on a Sunday, the dining-room was packed. It buzzed with lively conversation, now and then punctuated with laughter. Its big windows faced the promenade and the curtain of basking sea; one could also see the Moot Hall, probably an exercise in Victorian Tudor.

'Dare one enquire how things are going?'

Gently hunched and swallowed lager. Now it was Makovrilov who was listening, brows drawn in a frown, to something that Claydon was telling them. Capel chuckled, following Gently's eyes.

'I'll risk a guess . . . haven't you just been interviewing those three?'

'We've become acquainted.'

'The price of lunch on it that Stan is trying to touch the old lad.'

'Is it a regular habit of Claydon's?'

'Somehow, his conversation always gets round to it. Oh lor' – he hasn't tried it on you, has he?'

'I'm down in his books to buy a Suckling.'

Capel shook his head in frank admiration.

'He deserves a notch on his gun for that! Though I'm afraid – just between professionals – that Stan's troubles are far from imaginary. How is he taking things?'

'Not as well as Stoven. Nor as badly as Hannah's father.'

129

'Yes . . . her father.'

Capel studied the musician, who sat listening with drooped mouth, hands folded under chin.

'I'd prescribe a sedative if he were on my list . . . he's the type who might go over the edge. Though, looking on the bright side, that sort of person usually recovers from a knock the quickest. What did you make of him?'

'Much the same as you. Just now he's taking it on the chin.'

'Yes, and that will go on for a while yet. He should be lying down, stuffed with julep.'

'Perhaps you could advise it?'

Capel shook his head regretfully. 'He isn't the sort of man you can offer advice to. Anyway, now he's supping his drink, and that may assist his equilibrium.'

The waiter took their orders and returned with the hors d'oeuvres. Up the room, the Riddlesworths were already beginning their main course. She had her back to them; he had stared directly at Gently only once, but then his lips had moved, when, after a pause, her head had turned.

At the other table, it had been Claydon whose glasses had gleamed for a moment, preceding stares from Stoven and the musician.

And, at either table, a little silence had followed inspection . . .

'How do you go about a job like this?'

They had agreed on a bottle of Liebfraumilch, which Capel had sampled with cocked head before signalling the waiter to pour.

'It's very largely routine.'

'Oh, come on now! In that case, any fool could do your job – old Mutton-chops, for example. There must be more to it than that.'

Gently drank. How did you explain that mixture of observation, experience and psychology which, with a touch of something else, you added to the groundwork of routine? There was no method in it. You might as well ask a composer where he got his tunes from. Just now, in this room, what was it that was operating? Because, surely enough, there were things in train . . .

'A patient calls you in with a complaint, and then you apply a routine to the symptoms.'

'Oh, granted.'

'By elimination, you isolate the cause.'

'Well, we hope so! But it isn't so simple. You have to take into account the patient. Patients are capable of misleading doctors, even to the extent of manufacturing symptoms. They may also believe they have fabulous complaints and insist on having them treated.'

'So that, along with routine?'

Capel's grey eyes twinkled. 'I always knew you weren't a common copper! All right, I asked a stupid question that didn't deserve an intelligent answer. For that, you must let me buy lunch.'

'My patients can be just as misleading.'

Claydon was talking again to the musician, who heard him fork in hand; but it was Stoven who, an instant later, sent a cautious glance up the room. Then he too joined in the conversation, apparently firing questions at the bookseller. Claydon's mien was apologetic. His glasses kept flickering towards Gently's table.

'Do you know your patient in the present case?'

'My patient is Hannah Stoven.'

'Hannah – aha. Whose symptoms you know, but with the cause still to isolate. Are you near it?'

'I've got to know Hannah. So perhaps the cause isn't far away.'

'Not far away.' Capel's eyes were shrewd. 'I suppose I must accept that phrase as figurative. Yet you are such a wily bird . . and looking round this dining-room, I can't help wondering if it was by accident you came here.'

'Principally to get a decent lunch.'

'At one table her father, ex-husband, and employer. At another a man who was very friendly and who took her sailing alone on his yacht. You must admit it is suggestive.'

'Was she alone on the yacht with Riddlesworth?'

'Didn't I mention that yesterday?'

Gently drained his glass and helped himself to more wine.

'What about that other yacht?' Capel pursued. 'The one she used to visit at Harford?'

'We have made our checks.'

'I see. And is that laddie lunching here today?'

'Your glass is empty.'

Capel grinned broadly, and reached for the bottle. But now, after a keen glance round the tables, his stare returned more than once up the room.

Their food came. Gently's was a cod steak that had the delicate savour of complete freshness, served with a sauce flavoured with the fennel that grew wild along the coast. He ate appreciatively, with sips of wine. Capel, meanwhile, was dealing with a grill. Around them the surf of conversation grew louder as food and wine had their effect. Across at the table by the bar, only Stoven seemed to be tucking in with relish; the bookseller was picking at his food, while Makovrilov spent much of his time gazing up the room. There, Riddlesworth had eyes for nobody except his companion across the table, and you could see him sitting very straight, as though defying any eyes that might be upon him. Sue Riddlesworth, too, was sitting stiffly upright: the pair struck a curiously hieratic note.

What were they expecting? That at the end of the meal, Gently was going to tap them on the shoulder?

'I can recommend the peach melba, old lad.'

Capel was quietly taking it all in. Every so often his angular head tilted as he compared impressions of the two tables. Wasn't it so obvious what was going on? Clearly Claydon had said his piece to the other two. Makovrilov's stare was becoming ever fiercer as he eyed the stubborn figure of the Group Captain. Now Stoven was beginning to get apprehensive, was leaning across to murmur to Makovrilov. But the musician merely gestured him away. Like Riddlesworth, he was sitting up rigidly in his chair.

'Another drop?'

'Thanks.'

'I've got some Bruiseyard at home – their '79 is a good young 'un. Have you tried it?'

'Not yet.'

'Even your French wife would appreciate that.'

Was Makovrilov going to confront the Group Captain? At every moment it seemed more probable. The bookseller, too, was now trying to pacify him, perhaps scared of an explosion that would include himself. Why hadn't the foolish little man kept his mouth shut? His tremulous hand was on Makovrilov's arm: and he must have made an impression, because the musician's mouth was twitching, and suddenly his hand was over his face. He was crying again! But it was over quickly, and he used his napkin to dab his eyes. Then he seized his fork with a sort of desperation and pitched some food into his mouth.

'Hullo . . . what's that fellow's interest in Groupie's car?'

Capel's eyes had switched to the window. Out there a car had cruised by, to halt a few yards from the gleaming Jaguar. Its driver had got out, and now stood eyeing the Jaguar with calculated intent.

'Do you know him?'

It was Shavers, and Gently could hazard a guess why he was there. Shavers also had been putting things together, and probably asking questions in all directions.

'I say – would he be Hannah's friend from Harford?'

Capel was too sharp altogether!

'If so, I can't admire her taste. He looks like a lad with something on his conscience.'

Dressed in bomber jacket and faded jeans, Shavers did present a shifty appearance, the more so when, with ducked head, he prowled round the Jaguar like an intending thief. But finally he got back in his own car and reversed it into a slot; then lit a cigarette, and settled down to watch the hotel . . .

At Riddlesworth's table, both heads had turned briefly towards the window.

'You know, I've got the feeling that I'm sitting-in on something.'

Capel was quizzing Gently with amused eyes.

'You aren't about to make a pinch, or something of that order?'

'Let's finish the bottle and have our coffee in the lounge.'

Because the lounge was where the next scene would be played, if another scene there was going to be. The Riddlesworths had already risen and were making their way to the swing doors. Alert at once, Makovrilov was following their movements with burning eyes, while out in his car Shavers stirred and hitched up higher in his seat.

Did they know – or care, how many eyes were on them? Politely, Riddlesworth held the door for his wife; she drifted through it like a duchess and, without a backward glance, he followed. Yes, they knew – but they didn't care: that was the message of their exit.

'For some reason, I'm almost holding my breath.'

Makovrilov was trying to rise, but Stoven was preventing him. Both he and Claydon were talking in lowered tones to the musician, and Stoven was nodding towards Gently. They prevailed, and Makovrilov sank back on his chair. But he threw Gently a scathing look.

'Coffee in the lounge – with brandy.'

Capel sorted out the bill. The surprising thing was that all these little dramas had passed unnoticed by the other diners. The conversation, the laughter proceeded, and champagne corks were popping at some of the tables. People who knew Capel waved to him or called out familiar greetings.

'Shall we go through?'

Once the swing doors had thudded, the sound was reduced as though by a switch. At first glance the lounge appeared empty, just a deserted arrangement of chairs and tables. Then they caught sight of Riddlesworth and his wife seated at a table in a corner, he with an unlit cheroot in his mouth, she smoking a cigarette in a holder. He rose at once and came across.

'I would appreciate a private word, Superintendent.'

The ruined face, the tight-lidded eyes met Gently with complete blankness.

'Very well. Where do you suggest?'

'The other corner will do. Perhaps, in the meantime, the doctor will be kind enough to entertain Sue.'

Capel bobbed his head, and Riddlesworth led Gently to the far end of the lounge.

A faint tang of Turkish tobacco that pervaded the lounge must have come from Sue Riddlesworth's cigarette, and Gently's first move on sitting down was to fill and light his pipe. Riddlesworth watched him patiently, then pushed an ashtray towards him: an act of casual politeness that nevertheless seemed to carry a challenge. He lit his cheroot.

'No doubt I may take it that you have made progress with your enquiries.'

'First things first! It will save a lot of time if you can tell me where I can find your son.'

'I'm afraid that situation hasn't changed.'

'It has changed a lot, and will change still more if he doesn't turn up tonight.'

'I can understand your interest, but I can't help you. I have given you what information I possess.'

They were talking in low tones like two men discussing some interesting gossip, heads together, ignoring the clamour that came subduedly through the swing doors. Gently had kept his pipe in his mouth, Riddlesworth was drawing evenly on his cheroot. From the other end of the lounge they could hear Capel's voice and Sue Riddlesworth's curt rejoinders.

'As you probably know, I have asked questions at the music school.'

'About Mark cutting classes, yes.'

'He had been cutting them at intervals since the spring.'

'If I had known at the time, I would have had it out with him.'

'He cut them on Friday.'

'Because the tide was suitable, and we are in the middle of the autumn migration.'

'His dinghy was seen moored by Hannah Stoven's.'

'With respect, that rests on the word of a doubtful witness.'

'We have witness that it happened on earlier occasions.'

'Mark's isn't the only dinghy on the river.'

'Yesterday and today the tide was also suitable, yet Mark's interest in migration seems suddenly to have lapsed.'

'He may have gone to the Grimchurch reserve or some other place.'

'Then tonight he should be home.'

'As you know, we expect him.'

If Riddlesworth had presented a dead bat before, now he had pads and all behind it. With the pressure on he simply grew cooler, getting quickly to the line of every ball. You could scarcely help admiring him: thus it must have been when his aircraft was disintegrating round him, when with half a face and his crew dead or dying he'd held on, still making the right moves . . .

'At the critical time on Friday, a car was left parked near the spot where Hannah died.'

'We've been over that. It wasn't mine. I spent the afternoon in my study.'

'A white car.'

'It's a popular colour.'

'A new white car.'

'Some cars are new. If you care to look outside, you'll see a new white Renault. And I'm certain you'll know who it belongs to.'

'Mr Stoven has accounted for his movements.'

'And so, I feel sure, has Mr Shavers.'

'Why do you mention Shavers?'

'Because he is waiting outside, also with some interest in new white cars.'

'Last night you rang him.'

'And if I did?'

'You were interested in the name of a certain witness.'

'No doubt that is what Shavers told you, and you are welcome to take his word if you wish.'

'Are you denying it?'

'No comment.'

'Then I'm inclined to take Shavers' word. You were trying to find out who had seen the two boats together, and might identify the person seen near them.'

'Would such curiosity be unnatural?'

'And, at the same time, you were fishing for any gossip about yourself and Hannah.'

The commotion of the dining-room sounded suddenly louder as a waitress with a tray pushed through the doors. She seemed momentarily nonplussed by the division of her customers, then elected to serve Capel and Sue Riddlesworth first. Gently blew smoke rings, Riddlesworth flicked ash. Eventually the tray came down to their end. Riddlesworth too had ordered brandy, and he took a sip when the glass was handed to him. The doors bumped again behind the waitress.

Gently said: 'You were also fishing when you rang Claydon.'

'If you say so. I was certainly surprised to find you so positive that Hannah had a lover.'

'I find that hard to believe.'

'So you tell me.'

'She had every opportunity. From the yacht club to her dwelling is a short distance, and the moorings would be deserted for much of the week.'

'Opportunity certainly.'

'Isn't your son a member?'

'We have had family membership for several years.'

'When the tide is right he could easily sail down there?'

'Easily, though I happen to know he rarely did.'

'But you yourself?'

Riddlesworth sipped brandy and followed it with coffee.

'Occasionally I do use the dinghy – perhaps more, now I'm without a yacht.'

'Use it to sail where?'

'Oh . . . here and there. It's a bit cramped for a long haul. Mostly I take a trip down to the church and back, that's quite far enough for me.'

'To the church.'

'Yes.'

'Near the bit of bank that you offered to point out to Hannah's father.'

'I don't just recall making such an offer.'

'But he remembers it.'

'That's his privilege.'

'The bit of bank, you told him, where his daughter died.'

'From what you told me, I could easily guess where.'

'Where your son has moored so often this summer.'

'In fact, I may have moored there myself.'

He gave Gently a flat stare, then reached for his coffee and brandy again. Was he leading Gently, just a little? But he was a man almost impossible to fathom! The pale, taut, seamed face gave nothing away, no more did the hooded, yellowish eyes. Yet he had initiated this session himself . . . presumably there was something he was trying to do?

'Principally, what I want is to question your son.'

'I trust the results won't disappoint you.'

'Naturally I shall post men at your place to pick him up when he returns.'

'They may have a long wait.'

'You said you expected him?'

'I'm not exactly Mark's keeper. But perhaps I should warn you that on some previous occasions, Mark has gone A.W.O.L. for days.'

'Are you telling me he has gone into hiding?'

'Just briefing you about his habits. Ten to one he'll run into your arms, but this may be the odd time out.'

'In that case I would put out a general alert.'

'I doubt if a sprat like Mark is worth one.'

'To me, his absence is increasingly significant.'

'That, I find quite surprising.'

Someone had pushed open the doors again but, after a pause, had retreated: but in the brief interval they had caught the sound of Makovrilov's querulous voice. Had he been trying to get in? Riddlesworth's eyes had shifted for an instant from

Gently to the doors. Then he had shrugged faintly and gone for another couple of sips.

'Did you have something you wished to tell me?'

'Yes. But I didn't want to interrupt your questions.'

'Perhaps you'll be brief.'

'If you like. You asked me something yesterday that I chose not to answer.'

Their eyes held, each stare as blank as the other. But inside himself Gently felt a quick stab of excitement. Now they were coming to it! To make this one point, Riddlesworth had been willing to put himself up to be shot at . . .

'Carry on.'

'Yesterday, I hadn't spoken of the matter to Sue. I felt that she must know of it first since it touched her so closely. But now the matter is out in the open, so I am prepared to answer your question. You asked me if Hannah had been my mistress, and the answer is, yes.'

Not by a glimmer did his expression change, yet suddenly Gently knew he was lying. It was as though between them had sprung a certain field of tension of which their blank faces were the two poles. Yet, without a moment of hesitation, he produced the next question:

'For how long?'

'Since last summer. Since those trips on the yacht. She made me understand she was willing, and we moored up and went below.'

'And after that?'

'You were shrewd enough to notice the opportunities there might be. The Tower is close to the yacht club which, except at weekends, is little used. She kept our books, so I was never at a loss for an excuse to meet her there. Not that I was ever called upon to find one. I believe our discretion was quite complete.'

In other words, advance notice that checking would produce no results.

'Did she ever ask you for money?'

'No.'

'Did you give her money?'

'I may have done.'

'How long did the liaison last?'

'We agreed to end it a fortnight ago.'

'By mutual agreement.'

'She was always concerned about us deceiving Sue, and so was I. We agreed that, from then on, we would simply be friends.'

'And not a single person knew.'

'To the best of my knowledge.'

'For example, your son Mark.'

'Mark included.'

It was neat, it was probable, it left no loose ends: and had the air of conceding what Gently had suspected. Yet it was false. It fitted every factor except the important one: Hannah. Because Hannah wouldn't have accepted him. Face and all, he was too strong, too self-sufficient: not the type that Hannah would take under her wing, write poetry about, pretend to be a myth. It was Hannah who was telling him that Riddlesworth lied, a protesting ghost at his elbow.

'On Friday afternoon, where were you?'

'On Friday afternoon, in my study.'

'Where was your son?'

'I don't know that, but when he turns up you can ask him.'

'He was sailing his dinghy.'

'To the best of my knowledge, the dinghy was never out on Friday, my car was used only in the morning, and Sue used hers to drive to Thwaite church. That really is all I can tell you, however unsatisfactory you may find it.'

The complete tale. And one that would stick if Mark Riddlesworth was half as good a liar as his father – or if they failed to find him, and Riddlesworth had pretty well hinted that they weren't going to. Once again, you couldn't help admiring this man who studied his cards so coolly, who played them so immaculately, never letting a trick pass him by . . .

'If that's all, I'd better be toddling.'

'That's all.'

Riddlesworth finished his brandy. The swing doors were

suddenly busy, several parties entering the lounge together. He rose and collected his wife, who smiled a goodbye to Capel but ignored Gently; then, when the gangway had cleared, once more held the door for her.

Capel was shaking his head and grinning.

'There's a pigeon pair for you! But I thought the lady seemed a little anxious about the yarn you were having with her old man.'

Gently drew on a cold pipe. 'Answer this off the top of your head! If you wanted to hide out with a tent round here, where would be the place to go?'

'A tent? I'd try Foulden Forest.'

'The forest . . . isn't that a bit frequented?'

'Yes, but they let the replanted sections run wild, and you could poke in there for a month together. But hey – look at this!'

Capel moved rapidly to the window. Outside on the park a little scene was enacting as the Riddlesworths went to their car. Makovrilov was standing near the Jaguar, his stare fixed malevolently on Riddlesworth, and along with him Stoven and the bookseller, while Shavers had scrambled out to join them. It was all over in a moment. As Riddlesworth unlocked his car, Makovrilov fell upon him with hysterical reproaches, his eyes wild, hands flailing, tears streaming down his face. Stoven tried to intervene, but was thrust aside; Claydon was wringing his hands and moaning; Shavers stood by, eating it all up, an expression of triumph in his face. And Riddlesworth? He totally ignored them, handed his wife into the car, got in himself, started the engine and, so slowly, drove away. It was impressive. Makovrilov was left standing, his hands frozen in a gesture; then, still weeping, he ran to his car, jumped in and drove off after the Jaguar. Stoven jumped into his, Claydon after him, to follow in Makovrilov's wake; and Shavers was left gazing after them with a savage pleasure in his eyes.

'Sorry – I must leave you now.'

Gently hustled out of the hotel. At once Shavers ran across to grab him by the arm.

'Chiefie – I've been waiting for you!'

'Clear off, Shavers.'

'Yes, but I know something that you don't. It was Groupie's son who was with Hannah, and now he's sodded off no one knows where.'

'We know that.'

'But you don't know this. I've had a chat with Groupie's daily. Yesterday morning there was a fair old ding-dong in Groupie's study, behind locked doors.'

'Who told you to ask questions?'

'Listen, sonny came out as white as a sheet, then they packed him off with his camping gear, all this first thing yesterday morning. So what about that for a cover-up? Sonny's the bloke you're looking for. And Hannah's old man knows it, he's no mug, which is why he's off after Groupie now . . .'

'Just keep your nose out of things!'

'But it's my business too, Chiefie . . .'

Violently, he pushed Shavers from him. At the police station he found Leyston in his office, making a snack lunch of sandwiches and beer.

'We need a warrant for Riddlesworth's place – first, we're going to check that his son isn't there.'

'First . . . ?'

'If we draw a blank, then we're putting men into Foulden Forest. And right away, send a patrol out to the house.' Gently sighed. 'To keep the peace!'

10

And peace was apparently being kept when, a little later, they drew up at the house, heading a small cavalcade of two patrol cars and a minibus loaded with uniform men. The Escort and the Renault were parked close by and Makovrilov and his supporters hovered near the gate; but just inside a hefty patrolman stood rocking on his heels and gazing at nothing. Shavers was there too, watching events with sharp eyes, while in the garden of a cottage across the road a couple with two children were looking on with interest.

'Give the minibus the down to park at the Maltings.'

Because the last thing they needed was a show of strength! Even now some visitors, who'd been hanging over the bridge, had begun strolling curiously up the road. One blessing was that the press were absent, which they wouldn't have been had they known about Gently: to date, they had been satisfied with a cagey statement issued too late to make Saturday's stop-press. Without pausing, Gently drove through the gates, then dropped his window to speak to the patrolman.

'Any trouble?'

'Just the foreign gent, sir. Says he's the girl's father and he wants to come in.'

'No one comes in . . .'

'Hi up, sir!'

He had to move swiftly to field Makovrilov. The musician had seized on the momentary diversion to make a dive through the gates.

'Sorry, sir.'

'Take your hands off – I will speak to that man!'

'You can't come in here, sir.'

'Yes, I am her father, I will confront him and his criminal son –'

'Just take it easy, sir . . .

Struggling like a wilful child, Makovrilov thrust his face towards Gently's window.

'You are protecting him – why? Because he is a hero? Because my daughter and myself are not English? But it shall not be. I will have justice. I will talk to the press, to a member of parliament . . . !'

The patrolman eased him away, still shouting, into the hands of the alarmed Stoven, and in his mirror Gently could see the architect trying to placate him, while Makovrilov's hands weaved passionately.

Leyston said tonelessly: 'We'll have trouble from him, sir.'

'Then the sooner we clear up this business the better.'

'I reckon he knows how to make a stink.'

Gently drove on up the drive.

The white Jaguar was parked before the house, which today one saw to be a long, double-fronted building, built in yellow-grey brick with slate roof and tall sash windows. Gently parked by the Jaguar. Behind him parked a patrol car, from which climbed two detective-constables. Four of them, they marched up the steps, and Leyston pressed the bell. Riddlesworth, who must have been waiting for them, opened at once; in his manner there was not the smallest concern.

'Come in, by all means.'

'I'll just show you this, sir.'

Leyston exhibited his warrant.

'Understood, all correct. I hope I can trust you fellows to make a neat job.'

If it was his intention to catch them on the wrong foot, in Leyston's case he had certainly succeeded. The local man had been nerving himself for a rough reception and now he could only gape foolishly.

'Yes . . . right, then. Jackson, you take the outside. Miller, you'd better come in with me . . .'

They entered, but in the hall Leyston still seemed at a loss what to do next.

'This is just a formality, really, sir . . .'

'I am quite used to formalities, Inspector.'

'If I may, sir . . . upstairs?'

'It seems as good a place as any to begin.'

'Yes, well then . . .'

Towing Miller behind him, Leyston beat a hasty retreat up the stairs.

'A drink while you wait, Superintendent?'

You would have thought Riddlesworth was running the show himself; and perhaps he was. Standing there in his hall, he gave every impression of being the man in charge. For certain they weren't going to find his son there, either in the house or the grounds, while from a window in the hall that looked down the long gardens one could see the dinghy, sitting innocently on its chocks. No, he wasn't so naïve: the son hadn't come back. He would be sitting tight somewhere, obeying orders . . .

'I'll just remain here.'

'Do take a seat. I believe Sue is watching television in the lounge – show-jumping from Hickstead. Sue is an enthusiast, used to be one for the ponies herself.'

'Is your son interested in horses?'

'Mark's only other interest is a passion for old churches. I don't know where he gets it from – certainly not from either of us.'

Could it have been a hint, thrown out so off-handedly? But Riddlesworth wasn't a man to throw out hints. He was merely amusing himself, making conversation: rubbing it in that he knew himself to be fireproof.

'Then your son's principal hobby is birds.'

'Mark has been a birdwatcher since he was a kid.'

'Here, you have a wide variety of habitats . . . heathland, marsh, sea and forest.'

'All those, and a reserve at Grimchurch.'

'You will have arboreal birds almost on your doorstep.'

'Odd you should mention them. Only this morning I saw a green woodpecker on one of our elms – a warning, no doubt.'

'There must be plenty in Foulden.'

'Mark claims to have seen crossbills there, too. Are birds your interest?'

'Birds, and trees.'

'Then you've come to the right place to live.'

Impossible to tell if the man was fencing – his responses were so immediate, so unforced. Gently had an uneasy feeling that he might be giving away more than he was getting. What did you do to rattle such a man? He must have seen the little tussle down the drive, be aware that Makovrilov was waiting for him, ready at any moment to create a scene.

'Sir . . . if you will.'

Leyston had come to the stairhead.

'Excuse me.'

'Of course.'

And Riddlesworth actually moved aside so that Gently shouldn't have to go round him to reach the stairs.

'What have you found?'

'Come this way, sir. We've taken a quick look through the kid's belongings.'

He led the way across the lounge-landing to a door at the end of a passage. It opened into a pleasant apartment that was half-bedroom, half-study, with a window looking towards the river and the distant tower of Bodney. There Miller sat on the edge of a desk, rapidly leafing through a file. Another file lay open on the desk, and from it Leyston took a loose sheet.

'What do you think, sir – isn't this her writing?'

One glance was enough to establish that: the sheet was written over in Hannah's hand, and in a language that had to be Czech. It appeared to be a poem in four-line stanzas, each with a wavy line scrawled beneath it, and though the text was quite impenetrable there appeared in the title a name: Endymion.

'Is that the only one?'

'It's all we've found.'

'Letters – a diary?'

'Nothing like that, sir.'

But there it was: perfect and damning, a piece of evidence they could never have expected to turn up.

'Ask the Group Captain to step this way.'

At last, a card had come to hand! And catching sight of a family photograph that hung on the wall, Gently felt even more certain that he was holding a trump. Between Riddlesworth and his wife stood a slim young man, smiling apologetically at the camera, a fragility in his large eyes and in the delicate structure of his features. Yes, he resembled his mother in the fine lines of his face and his slender build, yes, there was a dreamy vulnerability about the gaze, slightly unfocused.

None of the others fitted as Hannah's lover, Shavers, Claydon, Riddlesworth himself; she had had sympathy for all of these, but not the tenderness of love. That had been reserved for this young man, solitary, helpless-seeming, shy, fearful of the girls of his own generation: Endymion, waiting for a hand to touch him in his dreams.

And if she had told him that it must end, just as once she had told Stoven?

'You asked for me, Superintendent?'

Gently pointed to the sheet of paper. For a second or so Riddlesworth stared at it, his face as expressionless as ever. Then his slit of a mouth twisted.

'Wonder what it says.'

'Is that all you have to tell me?'

'What? I don't know Czech, and Hannah would never explain it to me.'

'You have seen it before?'

'She gave it to me. It amused me to have a sample of Czech. I had some Czechs in my squadron at one time – they weren't so mad as the Poles, though not far off it. So I asked Hannah for this. Then I gave it to Mark, to see if he could make anything of it.'

The same readiness, the same blankness: but the same unmistakable tension. Riddlesworth was lying, and both of them knew it. A splendid lie, forged in those couple of seconds when he was apparently poring over the sheet.

'What does the name, Endymion, mean to you?'

'Keats and Disraeli come to mind.'

'We have Hannah's diary. She was having an affair with a man she called Endymion.'

'With me.'

'Endymion was a youth.'

'Don't think that would have bothered Hannah.'

'She met him first in April.'

'Another one of her fancies.'

'It wasn't a fancy that she thought herself pregnant in May.'

'That could have happened at any time.'

'They met on the river and made love on the bank where she was strangled.'

'We have been on the river together and moored to make love, though I have to admit that it stopped short of strangling.'

'And now we find this poem in your son's possession.'

'Only, as I explained, he had it from me.'

'While, at the same time, you refuse to produce him.'

'That is pure supposition, which I have to deny.'

'Will you also deny that yesterday morning you had a serious discussion with him in your study, and that it was not until after that he packed his camping gear and left?'

'Aha.' He paused very briefly. 'Since you know that, I certainly won't deny it. I was hauling Mark over the coals about skipping lectures, and he cleared off in a bit of a huff.'

'Previously you told me you didn't know about his absences.'

'Yes, well, they came to light yesterday.'

'I think perhaps earlier.'

'Say I had my suspicions, but yesterday he dropped something that confirmed them.'

'He dropped what?'

'Just an incautious statement. About being on the loose when he should have been in class.'

And suddenly Gently grew fed up with the game, which both were playing in total awareness. It was a waste of time! He had won his trick with Riddlesworth's first lie. Now nothing remained but to get hold of the son and to put him under the hammer: the chips were down, and Riddlesworth knew it, however clever his delaying tactics.

'Finish the search.'

'Yes sir.'

Gently took charge of the file and the sheet.

'Do you require a receipt?'

Riddlesworth shook his head as though that were a trifle not worth considering.

'I shall be leaving a man here.'

'Understood.'

'I would prefer it if you held yourself available.'

'I intend to.'

He saw them out, not closing the door till they were in their cars.

At the gates, Makovrilov started at the sight of him, and had to be restrained by Stoven and the bookseller.

The sun was sitting low as they sped towards the forest, which marched in a dark line across the gentle sweep of the landscape. Mostly sections of Scots and Corsican pine, it gave an impression of extending to great depth. The sections were solid, keeping out the sky, housing an underworld of semi-twilight.

'What are your arrangements?'

'I'm in touch with Ashbridge, sir. They're putting in men from the other side. I'll be dropping off a man at each ride, but we may not have combed the whole area by dark.'

'Are there any special areas where they've replanted lately?'

'According to the forestry office, mostly in the west.'

'That is where we'll concentrate the search.'

Leyston stroked a sideboard, and was silent.

So it was a gamble! But much less of a gamble when all the circumstances were considered. The forest was large, it was close to Thwaite, and parts of it were visited only infrequently. Riddlesworth would want his son quickly into cover, and in a place where he could reach him at short notice: where he could be supported from home, and kept in touch with developments. Where better than the forest? The son was familiar with it, and no doubt the father was too. The marshes were inhospitable, the coast exposed, but the forest answered all requirements . . .

'When do we start dropping, sir?'

'Not yet.'

They had arrived at a minor road striking into the forest. On one side recent felling had opened wide stretches, left guarded by a ragged line of pines. The vacant expanses were russet with bracken but otherwise offered little cover. On the other side, behind a colourful skirt of small beeches, larches and birches, the ranks of pine closed in; but there too the forest floor was sparsely carpeted, mainly with low brambles and pale-leaved elders.

'Does this road run westerly?'

'About west, sir.'

'How far?'

'A mile and a half, I'd reckon.'

'We'll start dropping men at the half-way point, but keep the dogs along with us.'

They drove on slowly, peering at the trees and at the plains of unkempt bracken, among which dwarf birches here and there raised little auburn pyramids. At the junctions of some rides a car would be parked, and they caught glimpses of distant walkers: not there! If one thing could be relied on, it was that Riddlesworth would have chosen his spot with faultless judgement. Though the sections of pine were gloomy, because of their naked boles one could see into them for a considerable distance. Gently checked his mileometer.

'We'll start dropping now.'

Behind them the patrol car and the minibus halted. So too did the other three cars that had been dogging them from the Maltings. Doors slammed, and Shavers hastened up, followed closely by Makovrilov.

'Chiefie, I want to give you a hand!'

'Stay clear, Shavers, or I'll have you arrested.'

'But listen, if the kid's in there you're going to need all the help you can get.'

'It is I, I who will lead this search!' panted Makovrilov,

shoving in ahead of Shavers. 'It is my daughter, I have the right, I demand to be leader of this search.'

'You'll both of you stay clear.'

'It is meet, it is fitting –'

'I'm telling you, Chiefie, I'll stay in line –'

'Shut up the pair of you!'

Gently eyed them fiercely, halting even Makovrilov in mid-flow. But then Stoven hurried up, eager to get his word in too.

'I really think it would be for the best –'

'This is police business and you will not interfere.'

'Mr Makovrilov is very upset, and I can promise that none of us will obstruct your proceedings.'

'That's right,' Shavers broke in. 'The old boy's in a state, it isn't human to stop him from tagging along. We'll keep an eye on him for you, and that'll be better than locking him up.'

'It will keep him away from a certain person,' Stoven murmured. 'If he goes back there, I can't be responsible.'

Something in that! Gently glared at the little group.

'Very well, then – get back to your cars. But you'll stay close to me and follow instructions, because if you don't I shall pinch the whole bunch of you.'

'I'm sure I can answer –' Stoven began, but another look from Gently sent him packing.

They dropped their man and passed on to the next ride, then the next, and the next. The road wound its way down a slight declivity and by verges of bracken and a pocket of dwarf birch. The low sun was still bathing the few pines on their right and setting aglow the yellow of maples, but none of it penetrated the chill twilight of the sections, where the pinkish boles stood together so closely. Now there were no more parked cars or any sighting of ramblers. Finally, they came to a wider ride, where a grove of tall birches stood pale against the pines.

'This is where the new plantings are, sir.'

Gently drove into the ride and parked. In rashes of stony ground and dead vegetation it ran away through the trees for at least half a mile. Sawdust around the entry suggested forestry activity, but the sawdust was caked and grey. Across the road from the ride was a thicket of young chestnut, now russet-yellow, and seemingly impenetrable.

'Put two men and a dog in that thicket. The other dog we'll take with us.'

'There's another ride further along, sir.'

'They can cover that after checking the thicket.'

He walked back to the three cars, which had dutifully parked behind the minibus. Claydon had ridden along with Stoven, and Shavers was now making one with the rest.

'Now listen! I want you lot to keep together and not to chase about ahead of the search. By all means keep your eyes open – we're looking for a tent or any evidence of an encampment. If you spot it, don't touch it, just report the find to me.'

'And if we see this criminal?' Makovrilov demanded.

'The same applies – tell me.'

'But if he is escaping?'

'He won't escape far – and what you won't do is try to arrest him.'

'But it is my natural right –'

Gently turned to Stoven. 'You, I am putting in charge of the party!'

He went back to Leyston and the dog-handler, whose charge was whining to be gone. They set off, with the dog ahead and Gently and Leyston working along the verges. Beneath trees on each side grew the low brambles and dead stalks of willow-herb and bracken still yellow, but as yet no cover that might hide a tent from a casual stroller in the ride. The sunlessness, the stony ground gave an aspect of wildness to the place, and suggested frost to come; the only sound was of their footsteps.

They arrived at a cross-ride, rather overgrown, and here the dog paused to whine afresh. It dipped its muzzle, its black eyes glinting, and struggled hard against the leash.

'Someone's been this way lately, sir . . .'

'Right.'

They followed the dog in. And now ahead there was a splash of weak sunlight, where the pines gave place to low, stunted oaks. It was a section, apparently, of neglected wilderness, where the bracken stood high as a man: cover enough. But there was no sign of an entry, and the dog stood whining and looking up at its master.

'Let him loose.'

The handler obeyed. The dog ranged excitedly hither and thither. At last it came to a little screen of broom and vanished at once between the bushes.

'Follow on . . .'

What the bushes hid was a division between sections of sapling pines, trees of only a few years' growth but set together as close as a fence. The gap was grown up with long dead grass, but plainly at times someone passed that way; and the dog was racing ahead enthusiastically, pausing only now and then to sniff.

'Look, sir.'

A patch of the fungi that grew everywhere in the forest had been crushed flat; and what was more, it still bore an impression – the splined print of a narrow tyre.

'His bike, sir. It has to be.'

'Call back the dog and put him on the leash.'

The quartet of irregulars were already through the bushes and advancing on them rapidly.

'Keep back, you –!'

'But that dog's on a scent, Chiefie –'

'Stay back as I told you!' Gently snarled.

Reluctantly, they waited for the dog to be leashed, then came on again, twenty yards in the rear.

Now the dog was panting and straining to get forward, ignoring the admonitions of its handler. Yet there was nothing to be seen ahead except tall, dark cliffs of fresh sections. The new plantings on either hand were opaque, choked with bramble, bracken and tangled grasses, while honeysuckle and Old Man's Beard trailed across the path to catch at their feet. Finally more broom scrub impeded the path, obliging the dog to pause and hunt; but then, an instant later, it made a lunge at the bushes and set up a triumphant barking.

'Quieten that dog!'

But its jubilation was justified. A few yards from the bushes they came upon the tent – a small backpacker, trimly pitched on level turf in a little amphitheatre. Beside it was propped a sports bicycle equipped with flasks and pannier bags, and before it, on a flat stone, stood a single-burner gas stove and kettle. Gently stooped to feel the kettle: it was warm. The flaps of the tent were taped back. But of the tent's occupant there was no sign; it might well have been a camp-site at an exhibition.

'He can't have got far, sir.'

Leyston too had bent to give the kettle a caress. But if the kettle had boiled, it could have been an hour since the camper left his site.

'Give the dog his nose.'

Freed from its leash, the dog sniffed around the tent with interest, made a couple of sorties about the site, then returned to nuzzle its master. Was it possible that Mark Riddlesworth had left by the same route that they had come in?

'So . . . at last you have discovered the assassin's hideout!'

Makovrilov had pushed through the bushes to glower at the tent. Behind him crowded the architect and Claydon, while Shavers had discovered a way in round the back. Makovrilov's bushy hair was dishevelled and quaintly fluffed with Old Man's Beard; he looked rather comic, so that you couldn't help wondering whether his passionate anger was entirely genuine.

'This you have found, but where is the miscreant? Why is the dog not set to find him? I think it is a game, a little trick, you do not mean to catch the son of your war-hero –'

'Hush, Stefan!' Stoven muttered. 'They're doing the best they can.'

'I do not think so. I think it is play-acting. I think they can lay hands on him this very moment.'

'Well, his bike's still here,' Shavers said. 'And he would hardly have bolted our way. I reckon he's out there in the trees, and if we get weaving we'll catch the sod.'

'Yes, we will catch him with the police, or without!'

'I'll bet he's stuck out there now, watching us.'

'Stefan, I really think –'

'I will catch this man, this killer of my child . . . !'

Just then Claydon gave an exclamation. He had been peering into the little tent. In it one could see a rolled sleeping-bag, an open haversack, aluminium utensils and other small gear. Claydon dropped on his knees and reached into the tent, then got up to extend a shaky hand.

'This was hers, I'm sure . . . I've seen her with it.'

What he had in his hand was a silver cigarette-lighter. Stoven grabbed it from him eagerly, and turned it over to exhibit an engraved monogram.

'He's right . . . look, H. S. This is a lighter I gave her one Christmas.' He tried to flick it, but the action was defective. 'The young devil must have pinched it from her bag.'

Gently held out his hand. 'Give it to me.'

'But this proves everything, don't you see? Hannah would never have given it away . . .'

Makovrilov howled: 'A thief too! Even, he stops to rifle her bag.'

'Just give me the lighter.'

Gently took it from Stoven. Clearly the lighter had not been used for some time. The silver was dull and had a sticky feel, while the movement was broken beyond repair.

'You have seen her use this recently?'

'Not recently,' Claydon quavered. 'After it broke she used matches. But before that she carried it in her bag, or had it on her table when she worked.'

'Do you see anything else of hers in the tent?'

Claydon seemed almost too upset to look. But Stoven dived into the tent and pitched the contents out on the grass. There was nothing anyone could swear to.

'Oh dear. Suddenly it brings her so close . . .'

'Let's get the bastard,' Shavers exclaimed. 'I remember her having that lighter, too.'

'Yes, we will get him – thief, assassin!'

'He'd have to go straight ahead, because of the cops.'

'If we spread out, the four of us . . .' Stoven put in.

'We'll have him cold, just you see.'

'Hold it!' Gently bawled.

But Shavers was already diving through the bushes, to be followed in a moment by Stoven and by the wild-looking Makovrilov. Claydon started to go too, but then faltered as though he felt the effort was beyond him.

'It's all so terrible . . . I can't believe it. Two days ago she was working on the books . . .'

'Give the dog a good smell of that sleeping-bag, then see if he can pick up a scent.'

The move was successful. The dog picked up the scent a few yards clear of the broom, tugging its master deeper into the section, through bracken, bines and the ubiquitous brambles. Had the youngster heard them coming, to make his retreat this way? If so, they might not be far behind him. And meanwhile, Shavers' voice could be heard whooping afar off, in a different direction.

But soon the trail made a sharp turn, perhaps where the quarry had decided that he was safely away; and then it took a straight line to the edge of the section and the pines where Shavers and his crew were cavorting. For what had he been heading — some definite objective, or merely the safety of greater distance? In that direction lay the heart of the forest, with sections extending mile by mile.

'Before long he'll run into the Ashford lads, sir.'

'Is there a road or houses down that way?'

'A road to the right, but no houses. The way he's going is all trees.'

They pressed on through the chill of the pines and in a light that was rapidly fading. From time to time the dog paused to sniff, but always to resume in the same direction. Behind them Claydon dragged along wearily, his short legs forced to go faster than theirs; ahead, they sometimes heard faint cries, now on the line of the scent, now wide of it. At length the dog began pulling to the right and they emerged into one of the principal rides.

'Sir . . . listen.'

Shavers' whoop was coming continuously from somewhere

in the trees on their left; a stupid, idiot sound that echoed strangely in the bleak air.

'Sounds like he might have spotted him . . .'

'Come on, then!'

They broke into a run down the ride, with the dog, catching the excitement, beginning to set up a furious barking.

'Can't you stop him?'

'He's a young dog, sir . . .'

Gently swore under his breath. Any hope of the fugitive's running into their arms had vanished with that savage noise.

'Look . . . there he goes!'

About a quarter of a mile ahead a figure had flitted across the ride, without as much as turning its head towards the men and the clamouring dog. Then a second figure: Shavers: followed by Stoven and the musician, the latter's thin body jerking puppet-like as he strove to keep up.

'Shall I let Rex go?'

'Hang on to him – he may nab one of the others!'

Distance seemed to stretch as they panted on to the place where the figures had dashed across. Here was another of the minor rides, impeded by bracken and trailing briars: They could see, far off, frenetic movements as the pursuers dodged and jumped over obstacles. Then came an angry shout from Shavers, and at the same time spritely notes from a car's siren; more shouting, the distinct slam of a door, and a sudden bright squeal of tyres.

'That's the road, there!'

Nothing could be more plain! But even the dog was too breathless to bark. Sweating, panting, they kicked aside the last briars to come out on the twilit minor road. There the baffled hunters stood staring after the sound of an engine fading into the forest, Shavers some yards down the road, Makovrilov wheezing helplessly, all three of them looking tattered from their belt along the ride.

'Who picked him up?'

'Who do you bloody think! His old man was waiting in his car. And I nearly had him . . .'

Shavers turned back, gulping breath, blood trickling from a thorn-scratch on his cheek.

'You will let him escape,' Makovrilov gasped. 'Why are there not patrols guarding this road?'

The dog had thrown itself down, to pant with lolling tongue, and Leyston was trying to raise control on the handler's transceiver.

The transceiver was beaten by the trees and there was nothing left for it but to tramp back to the vehicles, leaving Riddlesworth with whatever margin he needed to deliver his son to fresh sanctuary. There wasn't much to say. Even Makovrilov appeared to have spent his indignation; Shavers tramped in sullen, Stoven in pensive resignation. As for the bookseller, he seemed completely done in and barely able to drag his feet: no doubt the cigarettes had taken a toll of his probably never too-robust constitution.

And Gently was at fault! As they laboured through the dusk, he had few illusions about that. Trying to get a reaction from Riddlesworth, he had tipped his hand to the man. There had been a contingency plan, of course – with Riddlesworth, that would be second nature. If there was a search, his son was to fall back to a rendezvous on the minor road. And the plan had worked. After Gently's naïve manoeuvre, Riddlesworth had driven straight to the rendezvous, snatched his son from under their noses and rushed him away ... to where? Because the forest, after all, must have been a *pis aller*, a temporary measure for something more permanent ... and wasn't this a coast where foreign yachts touched, and fishing boats slipped out on nocturnal occasions?

Leyston murmured: 'The old boy was right, sir. I should have had that road patrolled.'

Or rather, Gently should have had it patrolled, since he had taken the case out of Leyston's hands!

'What do we do now?'

'A general alert for Riddlesworth and his son.'

'I reckon he'll be expecting that, sir . . .'

Did the fellow need to rub it in?

It was quite dark when, half an hour later, they arrived back at the cars, and Leyston could use the radio in the minibus to get the wheels moving again. Meanwhile Shavers and his mates hung around as though they too were part of the operation – privileged, at least, to share consultations, or to be informed of the next move.

'I had my hand on the door-handle of that car . . .'

Shavers couldn't forget his near-success. And wasn't he in particular a privileged person, a man who knew the game and spoke the same language?

'Anyway, that lighter will do for the sod.'

'She may have given it to him . . .' Claydon ventured.

'Like hell. Tell a jury that. You haven't been around the courts, mate.'

'If I hadn't spotted it . . .'

'Chiefie would have spotted it. With her initials on it and all.'

Primly, Stoven said: 'She wouldn't have given it to anyone. As a matter of fact, it had a special significance.'

Makovrilov wailed: 'But I do not care now! This young man has fled, and it does not matter. They may find him or let him go . . . now I wish to see my daughter. I want my Hannah . . .'

He still had the fluff in his hair, and one of his trouser-legs was rent almost to the knee.

Leyston climbed down from the minibus and beckoned Gently aside.

'Sir . . . here's a turn-up. The Group Captain is back at his house.'

'What!'

'Our man called in. Seems the Group Captain was away for a little over an hour.'

'He came back alone?'

'Yes sir. Said he was popping out to see the autumn colours. He checked in a few minutes ago, and now him and his wife are having tea.'

They were, were they! But one thing followed: Mark Riddlesworth must still be in the area. At the most, he was quarter of an hour's drive from the forest, which scarcely left time even to hustle him into Shinglebourne. So where was he? Smuggled into the house? But Riddlesworth would expect them to look there first. The marshes? Not much of a prospect. Could he credibly have doubled back with him into the forest?

'Do we get over there, sir?'

'Wait! I'm tired of playing the Group Captain's game.'

Because another thing had struck him – if he'd shown his cards to the Group Captain, hadn't the Group Captain given him just a glimpse of his own?

'Within quarter of an hour's drive of here, how many churches?'

'Churches, sir?'

'That's what I said.'

Leyston stared at him strangely. 'There's just Thwaite and Bodney . . . and Bodney hasn't been used for years.'

Had he hit it? He felt a surge of certainty, almost of exultation: of course! And suddenly he was quite positive that he'd locked on to Riddlesworth's devious mind . . .

'Send a car to Bodney Church.'

'Sir . . . ?'

'They are to collect young Riddlesworth and to drive him to the police-station.'

'But sir!'

'After that they can give me a ring – at Riddlesworth's house, where I'll be taking tea.'

He waved Leyston back to the minibus, then strode over to the gang of four.

'Right – the show is over!'

And he waved them to their cars, too.

'By chance I ran into my son, Superintendent.'

Gently didn't even bother to repress a smile – this was too predictable! Given a critical situation, Riddlesworth would always try for an unexpected response. He was standing before the hearth in his drawing-room, warming his bottom as he sipped tea, still acting the man in command even though by now he must be aware that the ice was growing pretty thin.

It was a handsome room, lit by subdued wall-lights and by a

standard lamp strategically placed. In a wing-armchair beside the hearth Sue Riddlesworth sat with the tea-tray.

'Could you squeeze me a cup?'

'I . . . yes!'

The wife didn't have quite the sang-froid of the husband! But she managed a tight little smile as she handed Gently his cup.

'That's better! Now . . . you were saying?'

Riddlesworth sipped before replying.

'My son. He's been camping in the forest . . . in fact, his gear is still out there. Quite by chance, I was able to rescue him from a rather nasty little incident.'

'More sugar, if I may . . . yes?'

Riddlesworth stared, but ploughed on.

'A fine afternoon, so I went for a drive – thought I'd take a look at the colours in the forest. As well I did. I came across Mark being chased by three ruffians – heaven knows why. I was just in time to haul him into the car.'

'He didn't tell you why he was being chased?'

'He had no idea. He'd just been rambling in the forest. Not the sort of thing we get much of in these parts, in spite of what happened here Friday.'

'Could I trouble you for a tea-cake?'

'What? Help yourself.'

'Actually, I'm waiting for a phone call.'

Now Riddlesworth was staring at him intently, almost with expression in his frozen face.

'Shall we have your son in, then?'

'I'm sorry . . . I wasn't expecting you back here so soon.'

'You mean he's still adrift?'

'I dropped him off in the village . . . though of course, he knows you want to talk to him.'

Another perfectly thought-out story, so why was it falling so very flat? With Gently munching his tea-cake cheerfully as though, on the whole, he couldn't care less?

'I've had a chat with Mark, you know.'

'Last night, in the forest, it must have been pretty chilly.'

'I suppose it was! But with regard to your business, chivvying Mark is a waste of time.'

'Shouldn't he be playing in the concert tonight?'

'What?'

'They tell me at the school that your son has talent.'

'What I'm trying to tell you is –'

'If you can manage it, I should love another cup.'

Hadn't Riddlesworth got it yet? His wife had. She'd been biting her lip and staring at the fire. Now she took Gently's cup savagely and splashed in more tea and milk. It was a curious moment. For once, it was the ex-bomber pilot who was being caught on the wrong foot. And he could scarcely believe it. He rocked gently on his heels, his lidless eyes gazing and vacant.

And just then the phone rang in the hall.

'It's Mark . . . you've got him, haven't you?'

Gently motioned Leyston to take the call. His eyes were on Riddlesworth's, Riddlesworth's on his as they listened to the Inspector's voice outside. Leyston came back: he nodded. After a pause, Riddlesworth put down his cup.

'You'll need me too.'

'I'm afraid I will.'

'Well, I don't blame any man for doing his duty.'

His indecision was over: he sounded almost relieved to be back again in a clear-cut situation.

'Shall I see him?'

'No.'

'Do I need to pack a bag?'

'If it becomes necessary your wife can pack one.'

'I'm coming too,' Sue Riddlesworth said promptly. 'Good lord, I suppose a mother is allowed to see her son?'

'You may not see him tonight.'

'I'm still coming. For that matter, you may as well arrest me too. I knew what was going on.'

'Then we shall need your statement.'

'But you'll have to wait till I've locked up and put a guard on the fire . . .'

Tonight there was only a thin mist hanging over the river and the road to the village. On second thoughts Sue Riddlesworth had chosen to drive her own car, and her lights followed them as they went. Riddlesworth sat beside Gently. He had nothing to say on the journey. There was frost in the air, and the streets of Shinglebourne looked largely deserted when they reached them. However, Stoven's Renault was parked outside the police-station, and he was waiting in reception to grab Gently.

'So you got the kid, then . . . I saw him brought in.'

'Have you something to tell me?'

'Yes . . . Stefan. I thought you'd like to know. I've persuaded him to take a couple of tablets and lie down.'

'Where are your other friends?'

'No friends of mine! Shavers cleared off back to Harford. Stan Claydon was with me till they brought in the kid, then he said he couldn't stand it and went home too. All that fellow's after is a loan . . .'

Stoven peered at the Riddlesworths, who were standing silently, grasping hands.

'So it's them too, is it . . . ?'

Gently leaned close to him to hiss in his ear:

'Bugger off!'

Then the Riddlesworths parted, still in silence, and the Group Captain was ushered away to an interview room. In the waiting-room he must have caught sight of his son, because as he passed it he gave a thumbs-up sign.

'If you would care to wait in your car, Mrs Riddlesworth.'

'Thank you, but I'd sooner stay here.'

Forlornly, she sat on one of the hard little chairs standing in full draught, by the door of reception.

So the scene was set: an interview room where the only furniture was a table and chairs, with a strong overhead light that lit the bare compartment harshly. Statement forms and a ballpen lay on the table, which was old, with a scrubbed top. The room was heated by an electric wall-stove which buzzed, and it smelled of disinfectant and stale tobacco smoke.

'Let's have him in, then.'

Gently sat behind the table with Leyston at one elbow; at the other sat a WPC, a hawkish-faced blonde, sharpening her pencils. Together they seemed to fill the small room, which couldn't have been more than ten feet by eight. When Mark Riddlesworth was prodded in by a constable he stood hesitating where to put himself.

'You go there.'

He sat himself awkwardly. He was dressed in a zip jacket and crew-necked sweater. His dark hair had got dishevelled so that a lock fell across his narrow forehead. He had smooth tanned cheeks and a high-bridged nose, and a small but firm mouth. His eyes were the same yellow-hazel as his father's; just now they were staring at Gently helplessly.

'Your name is Mark Riddlesworth?'

'Yes.'

'What were you running away from this afternoon?'

'I wasn't exactly . . . some people were chasing me. I thought . . . well, that I better hadn't hang around.'

He spoke with a certain boldness, yet that wasn't the message of his eyes. He was clasping his hands beneath the table and leaning forward as he spoke.

'We are investigating the death of Mrs Stoven.'

'Yes . . .'

'Didn't you understand that the police would want to question you?'

'No, why should I? No . . . of course! Not until my father told me . . .'

'That was the first you knew of it?'

'Yes.'

'But why then were you hiding in Bodney Church?'

'I wasn't hiding – exactly –'

'What would you call it?'

'I went there . . . I'm interested in churches . . .'

Did he even expect to be believed? His eyes were fascinated by Gently, appealing to him . . . but for what? Not to ask questions that he wasn't briefed to answer?

'How long had you been acquainted with Mrs Stoven?'

'I'm not. I mean, I wasn't.'

'Didn't you first meet her on April 28th, when you were sailing your dinghy near Bodney Church?'

'No . . . I've never met her.'

'That is the date she gives in her diary.'

'But it wasn't me . . . I mean, it couldn't have been. She must have been writing about someone else.'

'Do you know her handwriting?'

'No – yes! You mean that poem you found in my desk. Dad gave it to me . . . I was interested . . . she gave it to him, for some reason.'

'Why would he give it to you?'

'I've told you, I was interested . . . it was in Czech, or something like that.'

'It mentioned a name.'

'It wasn't mine. And it wasn't me she mentioned in her diary, either.'

'There are other dates.'

'I can't help that.'

'On certain dates you didn't turn up to classes.'

'Because I was birdwatching –'

'Yet your dinghy and hers were seen pulled up together, near Bodney Church.'

'No – not my dinghy!'

'But if the dates coincide?'

'I tell you – I can show you my notebook . . .'

'But if they *exactly* coincide?'

'It's to do with the tides . . . if they suited me, perhaps they suited her . . .'

The reason why the interview room smelled of disinfectant was because customers occasionally vomited, and Mark Riddlesworth's pallor, perspiration and swerving eyes suggested that he was about to join their number. The small room with its five inmates was hotting up and its atmosphere becoming close.

'Open that window a fraction.'

To get to it, the constable had to borrow Leyston's chair.

Then one could feel an icy draught alternating with waves of warmth from the buzzing heater.

'Let's come to Friday . . .'

Mark Riddlesworth wasn't looking greatly revived by the improved ventilation.

'Describe your movements to me.'

'I . . . I went to classes. If you ask at the school they'll tell you . . .'

'We have made enquiries at the school.'

'Yes, well . . . after lunch, I didn't have very much on. I thought . . . I suppose I shouldn't have . . . but with the tide at low slack . . .'

'You went out in your dinghy.'

'Yes, but that doesn't mean to say –!' He weaved a little. 'Actually, it's the autumn migration . . . though that may not mean much to you.'

'Where did you go?'

'Downstream . . . the creeks.'

'Surely at low slack they wouldn't be navigable?'

'Yes, but the tides are at spring.'

'In that case, wouldn't there be even less water?'

'I don't know . . . I don't know what I'm saying! But that's where I went. There was water enough . . . perhaps the flood was pushing it up.'

'At what time was that?'

'At three . . . about.'

'At three your dinghy was seen pulled up.'

'But no, it couldn't have been!'

'Along with the dinghy belonging to Mrs Stoven.'

'But I never pulled up there –!'

'Pulled up where?'

'I don't know . . . where you're saying.'

'Where was that?'

'There's only one place, isn't there? Above the church . . . there's nowhere else . . .'

'A place you know well.'

'No! I've never even moored there . . .

'We have questioned a student who says that you did.'

'Well, perhaps once ... I don't remember ... but not recently. Why would I?'

'Plainly to meet Mrs Stoven, whose dinghy was several times seen there with yours.'

'No – no!'

There was a real danger now that he was going to throw up over the table; he was trembling and listing from side to side, with the sweat standing out on his blanched forehead.

'Fetch a glass of water.'

The glass was fetched and pushed into the young man's hand. He gulped it noisily, then covered his mouth as though afraid it might not stay down. At last he sat back, partly recovered, and jacked his eyes again to Gently's.

'I believe you met Mrs Stoven, and that it was to have been for the last time.'

He shuddered. 'But I tell you I've never met her!'

'If your parents had met her, wouldn't you have done too?'

'I say no!'

'Wouldn't you have met her at the yacht club?'

'I scarcely ever go there.'

'At Claydon's bookshop?'

'I buy my books through the school.'

'With her father, at the Festival?'

'I was camping in Wales ...'

'But on the river you did meet her. On April 28th.'

'No – please no!'

'And on subsequent occasions. You joined her at the mooring above the church and went with her to a spot a short distance away.'

'If you're talking about the gorses –'

'Am I?'

'Yes ... where else would anyone go? Well, I've been there ... it's where long-tailed tits nest ... that's all, the only reason.'

'So you have been there more than once?'

'Yes ... I don't know! But not with her.'

'In October, were you looking for tits' nests?'

'On Friday, I keep telling you, I didn't go there . . .'

'Yet your boat and hers were seen there.'

'No!'

'And you were not seen sailing in the vicinity of the creeks.'

'I can't help that –'

'It doesn't bear out your story.'

'I didn't go there with her – I didn't – I didn't!'

'Then where did you get this from?'

Gently took out the lighter and placed it slap on the table between them. Mark Riddlesworth stared at it stupidly, shrinking back in his chair.

'I don't know . . . I didn't. What is it . . . ?'

'A lighter given to Mrs Stoven by her ex-husband.'

'But what's it got to do with me?'

'That's what I'm asking you.'

'But . . . I tell you, I've never seen it before!'

'She used to carry it in her handbag.'

'She never . . . I never . . .'

'It wasn't in her handbag when she was found.'

'But . . .'

'This lighter was found an hour or two ago in your tent in Foulden Forest.'

'Oh . . . no!'

'What I want now is for you to explain how it came there.'

If he didn't vomit it must have been because a fit of hysterical sobbing inhibited it. His slim body pumped with sobs that he was making futile efforts to restrain. But then he hugged his face in his hands and gave way to a rush of tears. The constable moved his feet, Leyston folded his arms; the hawkish blonde stared at the young man sulkily.

'Well, Riddlesworth?'

'I've got to tell you, haven't I?'

'That is entirely up to you.'

'Yes, but you think . . . you won't believe me! And I can only say . . . I can't explain . . .'

'Listen carefully, Riddlesworth. You don't have to say anything, but what you do will be taken down and may be given in evidence. Do you understand that?'

He gulped down sobs. 'Yes . . . I know! It means you have it in mind to charge me.'

He might have had the Judges' Rules at his elbow. Gently nodded to the blonde, who selected a pencil and opened her notebook.

'Very well. Now you can tell me.'

'If I may . . . some more water.'

Surprisingly, he asked for a cigarette too, and the blonde found him one and gave him a light. For a while he sat sipping water and inhaling, a little reminding one of the tactics of his formidable father. Was there a contingency plan for this too, for the moment when he'd have to make his admission? It was possible; Riddlesworth had revealed that he was not unfamiliar with courts martial.

Finally the young man pulled himself together.

'It's true, then . . . I was Hannah's lover.'

'It is you she refers to in the diary?'

After a pause, he nodded.

'You'll never understand this, it sounds too improbable, but till yesterday I didn't even know her name . . . not her surname, that is. She just told me to call her Hannah . . .'

'Did she know who you were?'

'I told her. But she wouldn't tell me anything. I guessed she came up from the town, but she wouldn't tell me where she lived. I wasn't to try to find out, either, or to see her anywhere else . . . we were just to meet, now and then, when the tide was right in the afternoon.'

'And you accepted that?'

'I can't explain it! In the first place, I'd never had a girl friend . . . and then she was older, and not English. I felt I had to do what she said . . .'

'April 28th was when you met?'

'Yes. I won't forget that date in a hurry. It was one of those mild days in early spring when just a few things are in fresh leaf.

It's true, I'd moored up to look for nests . . . there's always one at least in the gorse there . . . and the gorse was in flower, mounds of it . . . then she came along and moored up too.'

'She spoke to you?'

'She asked what I was looking for . . . I told her, and showed her a nest. It was queer . . . I don't really get on with women . . . but she was different. I can't explain . . .'

'You made love.'

'Well . . . she . . .' He squirmed a little and looked down.

'It was the first time.'

'You'll never understand! But with her it was all so natural. It was as though it were meant . . . as though just then and just there it had always been going to happen. I tried to tell her and she laughed . . . That's when she christened me Endymion. Then she made me leave ahead of her and said I must never try to find out who she was.'

'She didn't ask who you were?'

'No. But I told her, later on.'

'What was her reaction?'

'She just smiled. It didn't seem to mean anything special to her.'

'Yet she knew your father.'

'I can't help it. She never asked me any questions. Perhaps it was all a dream, like it was with Endymion. I don't suppose you're believing any of this.'

On the contrary: his tale had a ring of truth that couldn't have been manufactured. Anything else would have struck a false note: it had to be exactly this.

'Were you in love with her?'

'I don't know. I don't think she was in love with me. Otherwise . . . well, she wouldn't have carried on that way, would she? I suppose I was too young, she wouldn't have wanted me around . . . there wasn't ány future in it. In fact, she told me I was too young, and said she knew a nice girl who was more my age.'

'What was the girl's name?'

'Elizabeth. She was going to bring her along, but she never did.'

'Because the tide was wrong on a certain day?'

'How did you know that!'

'Never mind.'

Mark Riddlesworth stared suspiciously at Gently, then dropped his gaze to the lighter. The blonde turned over a leaf and made a grab for a fresh pencil.

'Well, if you know it all anyway . . .'

'When did she give you the poem?'

'I don't see that it matters –'

'Wasn't it on Friday?'

'I haven't admitted yet . . .'

He worked his hands beneath the table.

'Friday, then . . .'

'Tell me what happened.'

'I wasn't certain she'd be coming . . . she'd already told me it would have to end. But I went anyway. And she was there. She was sitting on the bank, smoking. She said that after this she'd be storing her dinghy so she wouldn't be seeing me any more. Then she gave me the poem, for a souvenir. She wouldn't tell me what it said. If I wanted to know, I was to get hold of a Czech dictionary and work it out.'

'Was that all she gave you?'

'What . . . ? Yes! You didn't think she was giving me money, did you?'

'Perhaps a token more permanent?'

'I gave her a silver key-ring, but those were the only presents we exchanged.'

'At what time did you get there?'

'At two or just after. I'd ducked out early from lunch. At first, she didn't say anything about not seeing me . . . it started off just as it had always done.'

'A visit to the gorse.'

'All right! Only this time it ended sooner . . . Then she gave me the poem and told me that this must be the last time.'

'And of course, you argued.'

'At first I couldn't say anything, just trailed after her down to the boats. Then I tried to get her to change her mind, but all she did was kiss me and send me packing.'

'You just went when she told you.'

'It's the truth.'

'She had smashed up your dream and you let her get away with it.'

'But I'd known it was going to happen –'

'She had simply been using you, and now it was no longer convenient you were getting the push.'

'But it wasn't like that!'

'Then how was it?'

'She was good to me. You don't understand! It was always as though she were looking after me, and this was part of it, sending me away.'

'Do you think I'm going to believe that?'

'But you've got to – I wouldn't have done anything to Hannah! She was just someone wonderful, I can't describe it . . . and now . . . now . . .'

His voice caught in a sob.

'So what is the end of this amazing story?'

'You can call it what you like – I don't care!'

'You just left her on the bank.'

'Yes, I did. Sitting on the bank with a cigarette.'

'Which she had lit with what?'

'I don't know how she lit it! But that's the last I saw of her . . . the last . . .'

He was sobbing again, and the blonde took the opportunity to make a few quick redactions to her scribble. Beside Gently, Leyston had got hold of a sideboard and was giving it little judicial tugs. Chummie was softening up! A little more leaning, and he'd be spilling it faster than the blonde could scrap it down . . .

Gently waited till the sobs had become sniffs.

'So what time are you saying you left?'

'I don't know . . . I couldn't have been there much longer than an hour.'

'You went straight home?'

'Yes.'

'What time did you arrive?'

'I don't know! About half-past three.'

'Who was there?'

'My father was there . . . mother didn't come in till later. I could hear father's typewriter going in the study, so I slipped upstairs and lay on my bed.'

'Did you notice his car outside?'

'It wasn't outside, it was in the garage. I leave my lifejacket in there, and I dropped it off before going up.'

'But your father was in the study.'

'Yes. He didn't come out till mother got home. And I was supposed to be at classes anyway, so I just stayed upstairs, keeping quiet.'

Did he have his father's facility for lying? Surely a little of it must have rubbed off! Yet you wouldn't have thought so, listening to him, to the young man thoroughly shaken by a police interrogation . . .

'Then on Friday, you say, you didn't know what had happened.'

'No.'

'Yet you knew about it early on Saturday.'

'That's because . . .'

'Because what?'

He had begun to tremble.

'Because . . . because I saw her.'

'You saw her!'

'Yes.' His trembling was pitiable. 'You see, I went down early . . . to the waterfront . . . to check the tide. And she was there.' He was holding on tightly to the table. 'I knew it was her boat . . . I could see it, coming down the garden . . . it was flood . . . I thought . . . then I saw what was in the boat . . .'

'It was on your waterfront?'

He nodded.

'Moored up?'

'No . . . just touching. There's the bend there . . . it had drifted out of the current and got stuck on our foreshore. And she was lying in it. She was wearing the same clothes. There were black marks on her throat . . . I thought I would faint.'

'What did you do?'

'I shoved it off.'

'Didn't it occur to you to go for help?'

He shook his head. 'I just couldn't take it . . . I shoved it off again into the current. I saw it disappear into the mist and then I ran back into the house.'

'Where you told your father.'

'I had to tell someone. I knew Dad would know the best thing to do. He decided I'd better make myself scarce for a while till we saw how things would turn out. So I took off to the forest, to a part we knew, where he could come and see me after dark. I didn't sleep much . . . being alone was ghastly. I think I would have given myself up, anyway.'

'We visited your tent.'

'I know. I heard your dog, and had to clear out.'

'You have still not explained how this lighter came to be there.'

'Because I don't know! If that's where it was.'

'*Have* you seen it before?'

'Never.'

'It could have been a parting present from her to you.'

'But it wasn't! I've told you about that. She gave me the poem, and that was all.'

'You wouldn't like to change your tale?'

'I'm telling you the truth.'

'And I'm suggesting you think hard about that.'

'I don't have to, it's how I'm saying. I've never seen the lighter before in my life.'

And his small mouth had set obstinately before he suddenly opened it to say:

'Are you going to charge me, now . . . ?'

Gently regarded him for a long time, while the heater buzzed and the blonde massaged her hands. Then he rose, picked up the lighter, and nodded Leyston to follow him.

'Let's go to your office.'

The office was chill, after the fug in the interview room. Leyston hastened to switch on a heater, but for the moment it merely glowed without producing warmth. Gently dropped on the chair behind the desk.

'In my opinion, the lighter was planted.'

'Planted . . . ?'

'It didn't come from a handbag. It's been lying about somewhere, perhaps in a drawer.'

'But . . . who, sir?'

Gently toyed with the lighter. 'It could have been in Claydon's hand when he reached into the tent. And a dud lighter is the sort of thing she might have left in her drawer at the shop.'

'But why would he do that?'

'Add up the score! Moulton saw a shortish man in dark clothing. Thwaite is on the way to Southgate, where Claydon turned up at four p.m. Claydon knew Hannah was going out in her boat, and may well have spied on her before. Time, place and opportunity. And now evidence planted in Riddlesworth's tent.'

'Are you saying Claydon's chummie?'

'I'm saying he fits.'

'But I can't believe . . .'

'What colour is his car?'

Leyston's sad eyes rounded. 'A white Hunter . . . it's old, but he keeps it polished like new.'

'Did you finish checking his alibi?'

'I haven't had time . . .'

Gently pushed the phone across the desk. He lit his pipe, blew clouds of smoke, and broke the match into several pieces. Yes . . . the bookseller! The little man with the invalid wife and housekeeper behind him, the failing business . . . and this strange, this reverent tie with the sympathetic Hannah. One of her lame ducks, like the others, but this one perhaps fatal in his inadequacy, clutching at the bit of strength she gave him, unable to tolerate the threat of a rival . . . She had been too kind! And her kindness may have killed her. Perhaps it had even been a fault.

'That's it, sir.'

'When did he leave the shop?'

'After lunch, he never came in at all. He must have thought you wouldn't bother to check.'

Shavers would have known better.

'Let's go and get him.'

There wasn't far to drive, just up Saxton Road, a bit past Capel's and the church. Like its neighbours, the house stood well back behind a lawn and frieze of shrubs. But unlike its neighbours, whose dark fronts showed only a window lit here and there, Claydon's house was ablaze, with windows lit in every room.

'Is he having a party, sir?'

It seemed unlikely. No sound of revelry came from the house. When they parked and cut their engine they were met by perfect silence. Nothing at all seemed to be stirring in any of those brightly lit rooms.

'It's a bit odd . . .'

Leyston rang, and chimes sounded emptily within. He rang again and kept pressing the button, but only the chimes rewarded his efforts.

'What do you think, sir?'

'Try a door.'

But the doors were locked at both front and back. Ringing, knocking and shouts from Leyston brought no response from the silent house.

'I don't like this, sir.'

'We'll have to break in.'

In his boot Gently carried a jemmy. Leyston took it and applied himself to the front door, which yielded smartly with a grinding creak. Then they were in.

'Sweet Jesus!'

In the staring light of the hall lay the body of a woman. Her blood was spattered along the wall and spreading in a pool, and she had horrific injuries to the head.

'He's gone mad!'

'Who is she?'

'I think . . . the housekeeper.'

Still there was no movement in that brightly lit house.

'I'll look upstairs, you search below.'

Gently rushed up tread covered with spongy carpet. On the landing a door stood wide. There, on a bed, lay a second body. This woman was wearing a dressing-gown: she had the same extensive injuries. On the floor lay a short-handled chopping-axe, its blade and handle drenched in blood.

'Claydon!'

No answer. He hurled open other doors. Then he came to one that was locked and launched himself against it, bursting a panel. Claydon was lying on the floor beside a bed, a glass, an empty bottle scattered near him. He was still breathing: his face was scarlet, lips parted over nicotine-stained teeth. His sleeves and shirt-front were soaked in blood, there was blood on his trousers where he'd scrubbed his hands, blood under his nails, in the creases of his fingers, on the glass, the bottle, a sheet of paper on the bed-table.

'Is he . . . is he . . . ?'

Like a chattering ghost, Leyston was standing in the door-way. Gently heaved up the bookseller and dumped him on the bed. But wouldn't it be better to leave him to die?

'There's a note . . .'

Yes, there was a note, scribbled in writing barely legible. Among the bloodstains it said: I loved her I couldn't bear it sorry please forgive me everyone.

Forgive him? Did that have some meaning? Hadn't Claydon killed all meaning?

'Ring for an ambulance.'

'I . . . yes.'

Leyston tottered from the room. Yet down in the hall they were in the presence of the woman who perhaps had been trying to escape when she was butchered. Rather than that the frosty night, the futile bells of the church down the road! He went outside, Leyston joined him, and together they waited for others to arrive.

And somehow – how? – he had to put it behind him, to become again the man whom Gabrielle expected: the husband she had left in England, whom she would meet on the platform, throwing herself into his arms with love and chatter . . .

How could he do that?

Claydon . . .

The blood he had spilt washed out the world.

'It's all yours to wrap up.'

'Yes sir . . .'

The first ambulance had come clanging through the gate, followed quickly by cars which, for lack of parking, were having to drive on to the lawn.

'Just thank the Riddlesworths for their assistance . . . the boy's statement you'll need for the inquest. Keep me out of it.'

Leyston seized his hand, but didn't say anything at all.

Was it he who drove the car? The next thing he remembered was driving too fast round the Ipswich ring road, looking for the turn-off to the station, and at least an hour too early for Gabrielle's train.

Claydon died. By the middle of November the smell of paint had left the hall, and on a Saturday Capel brought the quintet to celebrate a house-warming at Heatherings. They played in the drawing-room, though at first Capel had fancied the galleried landing; but that would have interfered with Mrs Jarvis's arrangements and had been vetoed by Gabrielle. The little concert began with gypsy music and ended with Hozeley's *Beach Suite*. At supper, Capel produced some bottles of the Bruiseyard '79, to receive Gabrielle's reluctant accolade. She and Tanya Capel quickly struck up an understanding, the more so because Tanya was intelligent about cooking; Reymerston was there, with Mrs Quennell, and Tom Friday brought his daughter, now engaged to Lesley Capel.

So the house for a while was filled with people and music, with conversation, toasts and laughter, and Gabrielle shone as mistress of Heatherings, the role she had coveted on first seeing the house. A happy woman! From the wings Gently admired her, so vivacious, so fulfilled: a queen in her setting. Yet wasn't she even more beautiful when, they alone, her face was for him only?

He found Capel watching him smilingly.

'Admit it, you think she's the prettiest woman here!'

'Well . . . don't you?'

'All wives excepted. If I had to start again, you might find me a rival.'

'Actually, we've been married for only three months.'

'Then I give you my permission to worship her. But not to keep her to yourself. She's far too valuable. You must let her light shine as far as Shinglebourne.'

Could it be for only three months? In fact he seemed to have known her for much, much longer, as though long ago her image had been planted in him, to come to life at once, the first moment they met. An absurd idea? But that was how it felt . . . only thus could he begin to describe it.

'Did you tell her what happened when she was in France?'

Gently shook his head. And he never would tell her.

'A frightful business. And I feel a bit to blame . . . I should have known that Stan was heading for a breakdown. I prescribed those pills.'

'You were not to blame.'

'Never be a doctor, whatever else. But I ought to have known. The signs were there.'

'I missed them too. Until too late.'

'Yes . . . but I knew Stan.' Capel's eyes puckered. 'He wasn't such a bad chap, either. When it comes to fellows like him, you begin to wonder whether some men aren't born to be victims.'

'To be them or make them?'

'It could amount to the same thing. But in Stan's case, you're left wondering. It might even have been a matter of hormone imbalance, and outside the moral field entirely.'

'Can you believe that?'

'You see, I knew him.'

'Just now, I think I'd sooner hear some more music.'

'Well . . . perhaps you're right. What shall it be?'

It was Gabrielle who decided on something of Fauré's.

But later on, when the cars had gone, and Gabrielle sat musing over a nightcap, she said suddenly:

'Aha! There is something I remember. Were you not to have bought that, what is it, a Suckling?'

'I changed my mind.'

'My friend, why?'

'It was an extra-illustrated copy.'

'And this you do not like? To be extra-illustrated?'

'Also, I thought the man's price was too high.'

Brundall, 1981/82

GABRIELLE'S WAY

Alan Hunter

Two seemingly unconnected incidents — the crash o
a light aircraft in a remote part of Scotland and the
kidnapping of a major French industrialist — bring
Superintendent Gently to the scene to investigate.
Only recently returned from France himself, he soon
detects the missing link: the mysterious Gabrielle
Ortec has suddenly disappeared from her Paris home.

As events of the 'Honfleur Affair' are thrown into new
and sharply painful relief, Gently tries to discover
what is really going on. Is Gabrielle involved again?
And, more important, will he be quick enough to save
her from sacrificing herself to atone for her previous
betrayal?

In a chase across the wild highlands of Scotland,
Gently must act fast — not only to save Gabrielle, but
to get to the kidnappers before his ruthless colleague
Empton precipitates a bloodbath.

'Hunter writes very well . . . Gently is always a highly
believable character.'
Irish Times

Futura Publications
Fiction/Crime
0 7088 2506 0

MURDER IN THE TITLE

Simon Brett

'Mercilessly witty send-up of threadbare stage whodunnits'
Guardian

Playing the corpse in a wooden murder mystery at the Regent Theatre, Rugland Spa, is not exactly a triumph for Charles Paris, actor: In fact his career could hardly sink any lower.

But suddenly the mystery spilled over into real life when a bizarre sequence of events culminated in the Artistic Director's apparent suicide. And the talents of Charles Paris, amateur sleuth, were called into action.

'every page is gentle fun'
Daily Telegraph

'the sounds and smells, the ambitions and frustrations, of a provincial repertory company . . . a neat homicide, and an economic, uncontrived, satisfactory solution'
Financial Times

Futura Publications
Fiction/Crime
0 7088 2520 6

PENNY BLACK

Susan Moody

Meet Penny Wanawake, philanthropist, free-thinker, part-time-sleuth. Very tall, very classy, very black, a beautiful tigress in tigress' clothing.

And her lover and friend, Barnaby, cool, witty, high-class thief, dedicated to the low-life.

Stand by as Penny meets Kimbell, black American detective, and blows his mind.

Thrill as between them they track down the brutal killer of Penny's wacky friend Marfa, and exact poetic justice among banks of orchids . . .

PENNY BLACK — the most dynamic debut in the world of crime.

Futura Publications
Fiction/Crime
0 7088 2682 2

TOMORROW'S TREASON

Palma Harcourt

'Palma Harcourt's novels are splendid'
Desmond Bagley

When scandal broke over British diplomat Jon Troy's head, his powerful American father-in-law was only too eager to hush things up – provided Jon agreed to a divorce and to being hustled out of Washington. Then the two men met again in Norway, where Jon found himself trapped in a network of violence, double dealing . . . and treason.

'A swingeing story set in uppermost American echelons and among diplomats in Norway'
The Times

'Another teasing yet totally satisfying "diplomatic" thriller'
She

Futura Publications
Fiction/Thriller
0 7088 2497 8

PEL AND THE STAGHOUND

Mark Hebden

Two notorious crooks involved in linked acts of violence; a third, possibly connected, repeatedly mugging homosexuals; and to top it all Rensselaer, a rich local businessman, has disappeared. Inspector Pel has enough troubles without his superiors in Paris decreeing more teamwork, computers and sociologists for the local Burgundian force.

Has Rensselaer been kidnapped – or murdered? Certainly his family is taking it very calmly. Only Archer, the wealthy man's favourite in his pack of staghounds, is fretting for his lost master.

'Maigret is dead – long live Insp. Pel'
Grimsby Evening Telegraph

Futura Publications
Fiction/Crime
0 7088 2488 9

TRIPLE

Ken Follett

The No. 1 Bestseller by the author of EYE OF THE NEEDLE.

'Sizzling narrative . . . One of the liveliest thrillers of the year.'
Time Magazine

A Jew, a Russian and an Egyptian meet briefly in Oxford in 1947. Twenty years later a shipment of uranium disappears between Antwerp and Genoa. And the man who returned from death takes on a mission that will lead him back into its gaping jaws.

'Ingenious, sentimental, violent . . . '
New York Times

'Highly imaginative . . . fascinating.'
Washington Post

'A compulsive page turner.'
Associated Press

Futura Publications
Fiction/Thriller
0 7088 1804 8

THE HOT ROCK

Donald E. Westlake

They stole it once, then they stole it again . . . and again . . . and again . . . and

It wasn't easy. First they had to bomb a museum, blow a jail, blitz a police station and break a bank. Then they had to heist THE HOT ROCK. And the pay-off? Well, that's where it *really* got difficult.

'Great fun'
Evening Standard

'Marvellously entertaining'
Irish Press

'Comes close to the ultimate in comic, big-caper novels'
New York Times

Futura Publications
Fiction/Crime
0 7088 2685 7

All Futura Books are available at your bookshop or newsagent, or can be ordered from the following address:
Futura Books, Cash Sales Department,
P.O. Box 11, Falmouth, Cornwall

Please send cheque or postal order (no currency), and allow 55p for postage and packing for the first book plus 22p for the second book and 14p for each additional book ordered up to a maximum charge of £1.75 in U.K.

Customers in Eire and B.F.P.O. please allow 55p for the first book, 22p for the second book plus 14p per copy for the next 7 books, thereafter 8p per book.

Overseas customers please allow £1.00 for postage and packing for the first book and 25p per copy for each additional book.